The Calibrated Alligator

and Other

Science Fiction Stories

By Robert Silverberg

Nonfiction

Science Fiction

ROBERT SILVERBERG

The Calibrated Alligator
and Other
Science Fiction Stories

HOLT, RINEHART AND WINSTON
New York Chicago San Francisco

F
S
c.1

"The Calibrated Alligator" first appeared in *Astounding Science Fiction*. Copyright © 1960 by Street & Smith Publications, Inc.

"Blaze of Glory" first appeared in *Galaxy*. Copyright © 1957 by Galaxy Publishing Corporation.

"The Artifact Business" first appeared in *Fantastic Universe*. Copyright © 1957 by King-Size Publications, Inc.

"Precedent" first appeared in *Astounding Science Fiction*. Copyright © 1957 by Street & Smith Publications, Inc.

"Mugwump 4" first appeared in *Galaxy*. Copyright © 1959 by Galaxy Publishing Corporation.

"Why?" first appeared in *Science Fiction Stories*. Copyright © 1957 by Columbia Publications, Inc.

"His Head in the Clouds" first appeared in *Science Fiction Stories*. Copyright © 1957 by Columbia Publications, Inc.

"Point of Focus" first appeared in *Astounding Science Fiction*. Copyright © 1958 by Street & Smith Publications, Inc.

"Delivery Guaranteed" first appeared in *Science Fiction Stories*. Copyright © 1958 by Columbia Publications, Inc.

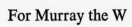

For Murray the W

Contents

The Calibrated Alligator

and Other

Science Fiction Stories

The Calibrated Alligator

Hydroponics technician Al Mason had been at Lunar Base Three long enough to be able to know almost intuitively when one of his fellow researchers was up to something funny. Mason had a natural bent for funny business himself, and he could sniff out a fellow culprit with ease.

Which was why Mason had been keeping a very close eye on Lloyd Ross, a recently arrived cryogenics man. Ross had come to Lunar Base Three on the July ship from Earth. He was a short, thinnish man with a limp yellow crewcut, and Mason had spotted something furtive about him almost from the start. There was something about Ross's eyes and about his reluctance to invite anyone into his personal quarters that led Mason to the instant assumption that Ross was up to something that was against the rather strict rules of Lunar Base Three. And, if there was any skulduggery going on, Mason wanted in on it.

Hydroponics technician Mason was an old hand at digging skuls himself. In the past few years he had taken part in virtually every jape, prank, and bit of tomfoolery that had gone on in the moon base. By far the most spectacular of Mason's enterprises was the so-called Project Bossie, which began with a bit of tissue from a cow's udder and ended in a monstrous mechanical and biological device that economically converted waste cellulose into a supply of milk and meat for the entire moon base. Project Bossie had been Mason's masterpiece. It was also one of the reasons why the high brass of Lunar Base Three looked fondly on him, despite his tendency toward irreverent violation of the base rules. The most important other reason was that Mason was a topflight hydroponics man, and his department was constantly coming up with new and valuable techniques. If practical jokes were the price that had to be paid in order to keep Mason at the moon base, the brass was willing to pay it.

But the furtiveness of the new cryogenics man troubled Mason. He hated to think that there might be something going on in the base without him.

Eight weeks of careful watching had confirmed Mason's suspicions without giving him any definite hints. Ross had a way of glancing around in the mess hall and then, when he thought no one was looking, slipping bits of meat into his overalls. What would a cryogenics man want with snips of meat, anyway, Mason wondered? If he needed the meat for some experiment legitimately connected with his research, he could requisition it openly through regular channels. But if he wanted the meat and didn't dare to go through channels to get it—why, Mason thought, that was a good sign that something peculiar was going on.

But Ross dropped no hints. He seemed to be a close-mouthed man by nature, who had made few intimate friends in his two months on the moon. He did his job, he played poker in Recreation Shed C a couple of nights a week, but otherwise he kept his own counsel. Mason's curiosity was inflamed. He *had* to know what Ross was up to.

One way to find out was to ask the fellows he worked with. So Mason buttonholed Len Garfield of the cryogenics staff after hours one day.

"That new fellow you have—Ross," Mason said, "he interests me. Is he a good worker?"

"So far he's been doing fine," Garfield said. "He knows his field, and he's making plenty of progress."

"And do you know anything about him?"

Garfield shrugged. "Only what's on his dossier. Three years of graduate work at the Harvard Low-Temperature Lab, then a National Science Foundation grant to come up here and continue his work."

"What's he doing?"

"Studying heat conduction in liquid Helium II. Thermo-mechanical effects, stuff like that. And, of course, he's looking into second sound and other temperature oscilla-tions. I've had a glance at his notebooks, and I'm impressed. He's got some completely fresh ideas, Al. You know that in ordinary media temperature waves are highly damped, whereas in Helium II—"

Mason held up a hand. Ordinarily he would have been glad to spend the evening discussing the peculiar properties of superfluids, but right now he had other fish to fry. "Okay. I'm sure it's fascinating, but not now. Tell me what you know about him *besides* his lab work, Len. What's he like personally?"

Frowning, Garfield said, "Oh—perfectly normal, I guess. A nice quiet guy. Spends a lot of time by himself."

3

"Meaning that you don't know a damn thing about him."

"If you want to put it that way," Garfield said, "I suppose you're right."

"Have you ever been inside his quarters?"

"Have I—hold it, Sherlock! You working for the Security Department in your spare time?"

Mason grinned. "I'm following a trail of my own."

"Well, the answer is no. I haven't been in his quarters. He hasn't invited me, and I haven't tried to push him. A man's got a right to some privacy, even in this overgrown goldfish bowl of ours."

"I suppose you're right," Mason said thoughtfully. "Well, thanks for nothing, I guess."

He drifted off toward Recreation Shed A, where a movie from Earth was being shown. Entering the shed, Mason stood at the rear, paying no attention to the film, simply waiting for his eyes to become accustomed to the dark. Then, moving to the side of the auditorium, he looked for cryogenics technician Ross.

There he was, Mason thought—fifth row, on the aisle. Mason nodded and left the shed. The bulletin board outside informed him that the picture would be running until 2200 hours.

About three-quarters of the staff of Lunar Base Three was at the showing. The rest were either putting in some extra time in their laboratories, or else were engaged in bull-sessions in the smaller recreation sheds. Mason wandered into Shed B. Dave Herst of chemistry and Nat Bryan of the solid-state team were playing chess; they were ferocious movie-haters. Mason waved at them and settled down by himself to wait for the movie to end.

4

The Calibrated Alligator

Movies were shown three nights a week. All in all, Mason thought, life at Lunar Base Three was pretty good. There were no women, unfortunately, though that was going to be remedied next year after the dome-expansion project was completed. But all else was fine.

Lunar Base Three was devoted to pure scientific research. The cream of America's college graduates fought it out for the honor to do research there. About half of the base's complement was there on short-term grants, ranging from eighteen months to five years. Others, like Mason, had won the right to indefinite assignment there.

Lunar Base One was an astronomical observatory, the best there was. Base Two was a munitions dump in which missiles and bombs gathered dust against the eventuality that the long-stalemated Cold War might suddenly become hot. And Base Three was staffed by researchers in just about every form of physical science.

There were five other domes on the moon. The Chinese had one, another belonged to India, and the rest were Russian. Outpost Lenin was the Russian missile base. Outpost Tsiolkovsky was the Soviet observatory, and Outpost Kapitza was the Russian equivalent of America's Lunar Base Three.

Idealists staffed Base Three, and idealists had invented it. The researchers had unlimited time and almost unlimited funds—subject only to the annual caprices of Congress. Even in A.D. 1996, there were some legislators from obscure regions who simply couldn't understand the point of throwing away billions of dollars on a laboratory on the moon. There were annual snipings at the Base Three appropriation. For that reason certain restrictions were in effect. Conspicuous waste had to be made inconspicuous, and conspicuously pie-eyed projects had to be kept under cover, for fear of congressional vengeance. Economy measures had to be observed.

Otherwise, though, the cosmos was the limit. And the men of Base Three, in their foggy-eyed impractical way, had managed to pour forth a torrent of highly practical inventions, of which Al Mason's mechanical milk-synthesizer was only one.

The movie broke at 2200, right on schedule. Mason came to the door of the recreation shed and looked out, hands on hips, searching for Ross.

At last he spied the cryogenics man—by himself, as usual —heading across the compound toward his quarters in D Dormitory. Mason nodded. He waited five minutes, long enough for Ross to enter the long, low hut. Then Mason trotted across to D Dorm himself.

He knocked on Ross's door. There was no answer. Mason knocked again, louder, and this time Ross said thinly, "Who—who is it?"

"Al Mason from hydroponics. Mind if I visit with you a while?"

Ross opened the door about five inches and stuck his face out. "H—hello. I'd invite you in, but my room's a mess. Why don't we go down to the recreation shed and talk there?"

Smiling, Mason gently shoved the door open. He was half a foot taller than Ross and at least fifty pounds heavier, and not even determined resistance could have kept Mason out. He said, "It's too noisy in the shed. Let's stay here."

And he was inside the room.

The Calibrated Alligator

Ross had gone white. Mason sat down and glanced around. The room looked like any other room in the jerry-built dorms—small, with a low curving ceiling, and rudimentary furniture. Ross kept it spotlessly neat, every book in place, every pencil on his desk aligned with precision. There was just one exception to the general neatness, and it was a glaring one. At the far side of the room a heap of soiled laundry was stacked on the floor. It was a startling exception to Ross's apparent love of orderliness.

Mason said casually, "Len Garfield tells me you're a liquid helium specialist. I'm interested in superfluids myself —as a layman, you understand; just an amateur's curiosity —and I'd like to talk about them a little. If you don't want to talk shop after hours, just say so, and I'll leave."

Ross seemed to be tempted to take the out. But, realizing apparently that it would be churlish, he said instead, "That's perfectly all right. I—I like talking about my work. What would you like to know?" He seemed frantically nervous. He kept glancing toward the heap of old laundry in the corner.

Mason said, "Well, there's this whole business of frictionless flow, for one thing. The uphill flow against gravity. It fascinates me. Could you tell me a little about it?"

Ross launched into a complex monologue. "To begin with, of course, you have to understand that liquid Helium II supports two different kinds of thermally-excited motions. We call these motions phonons and rotons. Phonons, you see, are quantized packets of Debye waves similar to those in crystal lattices. The rotons are rotational or vortex motions with quantized angular momentum, and—"

Mason's face was a study in grim concentration. He

frowned and grimaced and ground his forehead with his knuckles, and after a few minutes he rose and began to pace the little room, while Ross continued talking. Mason approached the pile of laundry. Glancing around, he saw sweat-beads pop out on the cryogenics man's thin face.

Mason said suddenly, "Hold it. You're getting out of my depth here. Let me sit down, then go back a couple of steps." He swung round and began to lower his two-hundred pounds of bone and muscle onto the pile of laundry.

"Watch out!" Ross screeched. "Don't sit there!"

Mason halted in a half-squat. "Why not? It's only a pile of old laundry, isn't it?"

"Yes, but—"

"It can't get any more crumpled if I sit on it."

"Please—it's a neurosis I have—I hate to have people sit on my laundry—"

Mason smiled. "Weirdest neurosis I've ever heard. Well, I'll just push the laundry aside and sit down next to it, then."

"No—don't do that either!"

Mason stood up. Slowly, he said, "You wouldn't be hiding something under that laundry that you wouldn't want me to see, would you?"

Ross goggled. "What—would—I—want—to—hide?" he said in a strangled voice.

"I can't imagine. But it wouldn't matter if I poked through it, then." Mason knew that what he was doing was a wanton invasion of personal privacy. But he suspected that he was on the trail of something more than usually amusing.

Ross let his shoulders slump. "You knew all along, didn't you?"

"Knew what?"

"That I was breaking the rules. I've seen you staring at me, spying on me. Well, it was inevitable that you'd find me out. Here. Take a look, and then you can go report me to Base Commander Henderson."

Ross scooped up the laundry. A glass tank about a foot and a half long had been hidden underneath. Mason squatted to take a close look.

A ten-inch alligator looked back at him.

Mason gasped. Automatically he quoted from the base rules: "Staff members shall not bring personal pets of any sort with them from Earth. Any animals discovered in the base will be confiscated and are subject to destruction."

"I know," said Ross miserably, "but I couldn't help myself. I couldn't leave the little creature behind."

"So you brought an alligator with you to the moon," Mason muttered. "Of all the screwball things—"

"It was a gift from my brother," Ross explained. "A going-away present. I've never been the pet-keeping type, you see, but somehow the alligator caught my fancy."

"How did you get him here?"

"In my allotment of equipment. I smuggled him in marked 'fragile.' Aboard ship I didn't need to feed him— they can go a few days without food. I knew it was a foolish thing, but, well—I was fond of him." Ross looked utterly shattered. "It's a shame that he'll be destroyed now."

"Who said he'll be destroyed?" Mason asked.

"Why—it's against the rules to have a pet here. And you'll report me, and Commander Henderson will take Caligula away."

"Caligula?"

"That's what I call him," Ross said, reddening even further.

Mason frowned. "The rule was designed to keep people from cluttering the base up with dogs and cats that might get underfoot and cause a general nuisance. Still, once you start making exceptions—" He shook his head. "We'll have to think up something."

"You mean you *aren't* going to report me to Henderson?"

Mason laughed and said, "Are you kidding? It's been months since I've broken a rule up here. High time I was involved in some mischief."

"I don't understand."

"Listen, Ross. I admire your spunk for smuggling this little green beastie up here. It shows you're flexible enough to ignore some of the rules that don't really matter. So I'm going to do all I can to help you out."

"Will you talk to Commander Henderson for me?"

"Uh-uh. A rule is a rule, and your pet would have to be confiscated if Henderson found out. So we've got to take some other tack to save poor Caligula here. When is a pet not a pet? Let me figure that one out for a while. The important thing," Mason mused, "is to change Caligula's status, and fix it so he's part of some important project up here—"

Within five minutes, Mason had formed his plan. He expounded it to Ross, who nodded with almost pathetic gratitude. The little cryogenics man had been frightened stiff that the illegal presence of the alligator might cost him his grant or otherwise get him into serious trouble, and the fact that the celebrated Al Mason was scheming to help him reduced Ross to a pitiable state of thankfulness.

Mason was amused. Caligula was an attractive little creature, with his beady eyes glinting up out of the tank observantly, with his blunt snout seeming to turn up into a knowing smirk. To Mason, the animal was a symbol of mild, harmless rebellion against a constricting and sometimes mindless set of regulations.

Ten minutes later, the number of conspirators had been increased to three. Mason summoned Ned Rankin of the biology staff to Ross's room. Rankin was an elongated scarecrow type of man, fiercely devoted to his work, and somewhat lighthearted about observing any of the base rules for which he personally had no use.

Mason had not told him why he was wanted at Ross's room. When he showed up, he was frowning darkly. "This had better be important, Al. Otherwise you're gonna be on my spit list. I was busy with—"

Mason cut him off. "Ned, you know Lloyd Ross of cryogenics, don't you? Lloyd, Ned Rankin."

The two men nodded. Everyone at the lunar base knew everyone else at least by name, if not more personally. Mason said, "Ned, I think you ought to know right at the start that Lloyd here has violated a base rule."

"So what? Is this a kangaroo court?"

"I just wanted to make it clear. We're going to take you into our confidence," Mason said. "If I didn't think I could trust you, I wouldn't have asked you over here. Ross, show him Caligula." Carefully Ross lifted the bundle of laundry, revealing the tank. Rankin unlimbered himself, strode over, peered down from his six-feet-five. He blinked.

11

"An *alligator?*"

"That's right," Mason said. "An alligator. It's a pet of our friend here. He was so fond of the critter that he couldn't bring himself to leave him behind on Earth, so he smuggled him in."

Rankin began to laugh. He scooped the alligator out of the tank, placed him on the palm of one enormous hand, and tickled him under the chin. Legs kicked in various directions. The tiny jaws clashed menacingly on emptiness. Rankin dropped Caligula back in his tank.

"Cute," he said. "Did you call me all the way over here to look at an alligator?"

Mason nodded. "As it stands now, the alligator is Ross's responsibility. And pets are strictly *verboten* up here, as you know. But Ross here would be heartbroken if the C.O. disposed of little Caligula. So it occurred to me that we could ensure the 'gator's continued good health by making him part of some official project up here. Maybe some project of the biology department. I seem to remember that a couple of months back you were talking, Ned, about importing some baby reptiles for a growth-acceleration project you had in mind—"

The beanpole biologist frowned. "Yes, but I wasn't planning to get started on that project for another six or eight months—"

"It wouldn't upset you too much to change your schedule, would it?"

"I suppose not," Rankin said thoughtfully. "Let me see, now—"

Ross spoke up. "Would you mind telling me what this project is, Dr. Rankin?"

"Well," Rankin said, "it's all based on the desire to make

12

the lunar base self-sufficient foodwise. We're already growing all our own vegetables, thanks largely to Mason here
and his hydroponics department. And we get milk and liver
from the artificial cow, also thanks to Mason. But the big
problem is obtaining other kinds of fresh meat. We don't
have room for a stable up here, you understand."

"Naturally."

"But," Rankin went on, "there is one life-form that is
potentially feasible for being farmed here. That would be
an herbivorous reptile."

"Reptile? You mean you'd have us eating alligators?"

Rankin grinned, "No, not alligators. Caligula is safe.
Alligator meat isn't the tastiest in the world—and anyway,
alligators are carnivorous, which makes them inefficient as
meat sources. But an herbivorous reptile has all sorts of
special advantages efficiencywise." Rankin ticked them off
on his fingers. "Since they're herbivorous, they don't require a feedback of meat; they can get along on spare prod-
uce from hydroponics. Since reptiles are somnolent, they
don't dissipate valuable energies in wandering around, graz-
ing, walking, things like that. They just lie still. Further-
more, being cold-blooded, they would thrive up here, where
the temperature is constant. The biggest hindrance to reptile
growth is sudden temperature change—but there's none of
that here. Fourthly, they're hatched from eggs—which
means a great many offspring at a time and no prolonged
period of prenatal care for the mother. Fifthly, they grow
fast. Unfortunately, not quite fast enough. But that last can
be remedied."

"But *are* there such herbivorous reptiles?" Ross asked.
"And can they be eaten?"

"The answers are yes and yes, emphatically. The iguana,

13

for instance—gets along quite well munching celery and lettuce, with a couple of bananas thrown in for variety. Requires no particular care, just lies still and grows to a length of about four feet. And the meat is delicious—a rare delicacy in South America, I understand. Considered more tasty than chicken."

"I still don't understand what my alligator has to do with this, though."

Mason said, "Rankin has been doodling up a process that accelerates the growth of reptiles, you see. It takes an iguana years to reach a length of four feet. If that process could be speeded up—say, to one year, or six months—we could keep a couple of tanksful of the critters here and use them for Sunday dinner."

"Exactly," Rankin said. "So far my growth-acceleration technique is strictly theoretical. I was planning to ask for an appropriation in a couple of months, requisition a few iguanas from Earth, and get started. But now's as good a time as any. And I can use this alligator as my first experimental animal. He won't be edible, of course, but he'll help to prove the general utility of the process. After that I can apply it to edible herbivores. And in the meanwhile we'll have saved Caligula from a horrible fate, and you from a reprimand."

"What is this process?" Ross asked uneasily.

"What it involves," Rankin said, "is biochemical growth stimulation. Give the alligator optimum living conditions, for one thing. Then apply treatment. Antibiotics, hormones, the works. An alligator normally grows at a rate of one inch per month. So we take Caligula here and fix up a little niche for him in my bio lab, and we see how fast we can

14

make him grow. If he responds, we know the treatment is useful. We can start raising iguanas up here, combining my treatment and some selective breeding to get them to size, and Lunar Base Three has a dandy new source of food."

"Not only Lunar Base Three, of course," Mason put in. "It's fine for us, but it's a lot more important for our employer down there—the five billion people of Earth. It'll be a really major breakthrough in terrestrial food supply. Not to mention the future potentiality when we start colonizing the planets."

"But if you put the alligator in your lab, I won't be able to see him," Ross objected.

"Sure you will," Mason said. "Ned will let you visit him whenever you want. Which is better, anyway, an alligator living in the bio lab, or one who gets confiscated and fed into the garbage converter?"

Ross gulped. "I see what you mean."

"There's one problem," Rankin said. "I can't very well begin the project unless I have some way of accounting for the presence of the alligator up here. Suppose Henderson wanders in and sees the creature, and wants to know how he got here? Am I supposed to tell him that he was smuggled up by Ross?"

Mason smiled confidently. "Never fear. I'll handle that part."

The next day, Mason wandered over to the administration hut during his lunch break. He sauntered casually past the base commander's office, which was unoccupied at the time, and entered the office of the Requisition Department.

The Calibrated Alligator

Sam Donohue, the Chief Requisition Clerk, was out of the office. It was just as well, Mason thought, for that meant that his assistant, Harry Gardner, would be in charge.

Gardner looked up from a forest of paperwork. "Anything I can do for you, Al?"

"Matter of fact, there is. I want you to make an ex post facto requisition for me."

Gardner's watery eyes bugged with puzzlement. "Huh?"

Mason leaned down low over the requisition clerk's desk and whispered hoarsely, "I want you to make an addition to the June requisition list."

"But that was months ago, Al. What good would it do if—"

Mason drummed his fingers on the desk. "I'd like you to correct an irregularity for me. Something was brought in on the July ship without being requisitioned. We have to juggle things so it looks legit."

"You mean, something was *smuggled* in?"

"Indeed something was," Mason said. "You and I both know that we can't allow smuggling up here. So get the June requisition list out and let's fix things up right now."

Gardner shook his head. "That wouldn't be right, Al," he said dimly.

Mason favored the clerk with a cold smile. "How would you like it if the C.O. found out that you used the taxpayers' money to ship twelve ounces of lunar pumice to a girlfriend of yours in Fond du Lac, Wisconsin, Harry?"

Gardner gaped. "How did you find out about—"

"It helps to have quick eyes," Mason said. "I saw the package being loaded, and I knew what was stamped on it. You finagled that package out of here postpaid, strictly

16

against regs, and charged thirty bucks' shipping costs off to the general expense fund."

"But everyone does that, Al!" Gardner said weakly.

"That doesn't excuse you," Mason snapped.

Gardner looked like a gaffed fish. He made a few more feeble attempts to wriggle, then gave up and dug into the files for the master copy of the June requisition sheet.

"Here are the filled-in requisitions," Mason said mercilessly. "Signed by Rankin of biology."

Gardner riffled through the triplicate blanks. "One live baby alligator?" he said faintly. "But—"

"Never mind. Insert it."

The master requisition list had already been gone over by Commander Henderson and bore his initials. It was strictly unkosher to add anything to the list after it had been signed. But Gardner found a blank space and obediently typed in the alligator requisition. Then he inked in the official goods-received voucher next to it.

"Fine," Mason said. "Now file everything away and forget everything that just happened. When Henderson starts wondering how the deuce an alligator got to the moon, we can dig this out and prove that he okayed the requisition himself."

Gardner looked dazed and glassy-eyed. "Sure, Al. Sure. Uh—you won't say anything about that box of pumice—"

"Not this time," Mason said. "I'll save it until the next time I need a favor. So long, Harry."

So it was all duly arranged, as Mason reported back to Ross and Rankin. Thanks to the chicanery in the requisitions office, Ross could no longer be accused of smuggling

Caligula into the base. It was demonstrable that Rankin had requisitioned one alligator in June, and that the animal had duly been shipped and had arrived along with Ross on the July ship. Naturally, there would be no record of the shipment on any of the Earthside documents nor on the cargo manifest of the Earth-Moon ship. But it was not likely that Commander Henderson would go to the trouble and expense of checking the Earthside documents. If he happened to bridle at the presence of the alligator in the bio lab, Rankin could maintain that he had requisitioned it months before for legitimate research purposes, and the Commander would have his own initials on the requisition sheet to prove it.

The paperwork taken care of, Caligula was duly transferred from his hiding place in Ross's quarters to an inconspicuous corner of Rankin's cluttered laboratory.

Ross looked doubtfully at the alligator's tank. "You aren't going to harm him in any way, are you?" he asked Rankin nervously.

The biologist scowled. "My friend, don't you see that my scientific reputation depends on keeping this scrawny little reptile alive and healthy?"

"Still, all this apparatus—"

"Necessary for measurements," Rankin said. He looked in appeal at Mason. "Al, will you vouch for the fact that this alligator is going to get the best of care here?"

"Sure," Mason said reassuringly to Ross. "Let me tell you—Rankin's going to treat Caligula the way he would probably treat his own child. Better, perhaps."

Ross nodded. "I'm not really worried. I'm just naturally pessimistic, I suppose."

"And now," Rankin said, "if you two will clear out of here and let me get my work started—"

Mason and Ross returned to the biology lab later in the day. By that time, Rankin had already surrounded the tank with an elaborate and impressive array of equipment. And the biologist had the pleasantly frayed expression that implied he had put in a busy day.

"Well?" Mason asked.

"I'm getting under way," Rankin said. "First step is to assure optimum temperature for growth. If the tank and environment's too cold, the alligator becomes torpid; doesn't grow. If it's too hot, he'll go dormant too. The trick is to keep his environment at just the precise temperature for maximum stimulation.

"Antibiotic treatment comes next. I've got half a dozen different things I want to try. They've all worked as growth stimulants in the past on other creatures. I'll work them in one at a time, starting with hydroxyphenylarsonic acid. Then there's the hormone treatment too, and some other things."

"What about food?"

"I've arranged it with the kitchen; they'll give me all the meat I want, from that cow of yours."

Mason peered into the tank. The alligator was paddling slowly up and down, looking cozy and contented. Ross looked in too. The man was positively beaming, Mason thought. He shrugged; there were those who loved cats and those who loved dogs, but he hadn't figured it was possible to work up much of an affection for an alligator.

"How—large will he get?" Ross asked.

"That's one of the questions I mean to answer with this experiment," said Rankin. "You know, theoretically a reptile can keep on growing just about forever, if he gets enough food and has optimum climate. We're in a position to supply both here. But I'm not so much interested in how big Caligula gets, as in how fast he grows."

Mason nodded. "Be careful not to turn him into a blasted dinosaur. He could start getting cumbersome after he hits the forty-foot mark."

Ross looked apprehensive. "It's too bad alligators have to grow up, isn't it?" he said. "They look so cute when they're this size."

"Thank you, J. M. Barrie," Mason said acidly. "I suppose you wish Rankin here was experimenting with a growth *inhibiting* process, instead of an accelerating one."

Ross smiled wistfully. "That would be nice, I suppose. But I mustn't be silly about this. I've got to thank you for taking me off the hook, Mr. Mason."

"Don't mention it, son. You gave me a chance to mess around with the regulations, and I'm always grateful for the opportunity to have some fun. Let's get out of here now. Rankin looks busy."

"I'm going to take measurements," the biologist announced. "I'll keep a daily record of growth. Let's see, now —September 17, 1996, length twenty-seven centimeters from snout to tail—"

Mason laughed. "The Calibrated Alligator! Science, it's wonderful!"

For the next few weeks, Mason paid frequent visits to the biology lab to see how Caligula was coming along. And the alligator's progress was, to say the least, alarming. Rankin waxed rhapsodic over the success of his various growth-stimulation notions. And Caligula was growing, if not precisely while one watched, then almost as fast. Rankin's process had galvanized the animal into expansion.

After the first month of life in the laboratory, Caligula had grown not the expected inch, but two and a half. During his second month of laboratory life that rate was exceeded; he added slightly more than three inches to his length, and now was no longer quite so cute and lovable-looking as he had been when his total body length was ten inches, tail included.

As the novelty of visiting the animal wore off, Mason's visits became less and less frequent. As a result, the increased size of the alligator was startling in the extreme whenever he did go to see the animal. It was difficult now to picture Caligula as he had been at his tiniest. By the time five months had gone by, he had more than doubled his length, had required a shift to a larger tank, and was starting to look slightly formidable.

"I've got him on a high calcium diet," Rankin explained. "Otherwise his bones would be too weak to support him, at the rate he's growing."

"How much does he eat?"

Rankin shrugged. "About as much as he can get. It's about time for feeding him, anyway."

From a small refrigerator, the biologist produced a chunk of meat that had evidently been sawed from the proliferating tissue-culture growth of Mason's milk-producing machine. Rankin dropped the chunk into the water of Caligula's tank. The alligator had been "sunning" himself on a rock beneath an ultraviolet lamp that Rankin had rigged.

Caligula glared at the chunk of meat for a long moment. His protruding eyes were fixed glassily on it.

His snout opened suddenly. Mason heard a chumping noise, and abruptly the meat no longer was in the water.

"He'd eat a chunk the size of my fist, if I gave it to him," Rankin said with a kind of pride.

"Does Ross come here often?"

"Every night," Rankin said. "But he looks a little dazed. I don't think that poor kid was really expecting his alligator to grow up at all."

Mason snorted. "There are times when I suspect that Ross hasn't grown up at all, himself. But they tell me he's a hell of a good cryogenics man, so I suppose he's entitled to go goofy over a reptile." He peered at the sleek brown alligator, remembering the time when Rankin had held him on the palm of one hand. It wouldn't be wise to try that now, not with the alligator better than two feet in length.

"Has Commander Henderson seen it?"

Rankin shook his head. "The commander hasn't been in this particular wing of the lab for months, thank goodness." Rankin began to giggle. "Lord, I hope he keeps out of here for about six more months!"

"Why?"

"By that time Caligula ought to be about four feet long," Rankin explained. "I want to see the look on the C.O.'s face when he finds four feet of alligator in his biology lab!"

During the next few months, Mason had little time to spend visiting the alligator, and rapidly Caligula slipped from his mind. He was busy with his own work, which included five or six major hydroponics projects and several dozen minor ones—and, besides operating in his specialty, he had the extra job of coordinating the team that was designing an improved and more efficient Bossie. The original milk-converter had been built by ear, so to speak, with improvised attachments surreptitiously added as they became necessary. But Henderson had been so impressed with the result that he had commissioned Mason to build a new Bossie, this time working from the ground up and perhaps avoiding a few of the drawbacks of the Mark I model.

The multiple jobs kept Mason busy—so busy that he forgot all about Caligula. From time to time he would run into Ned Rankin, who would give him a progress report—"Still growing," or words to that effect. Mason would nod and say, "That's nice," or words to that effect.

Time passed, and it was now a year since Rankin had begun the alligator-augmentation project. It was late one afternoon; Mason was busy in his hydroponics lab, breaking in a couple of kids newly arrived from Earth, and it was only when Mason saw the pale and puzzled faces of his apprentices that he realized someone had been standing behind him.

Mason turned and found himself staring into the lean, alert face of Base Commander Henderson. Mason double took, recovering balance reasonably swiftly.

"H-hello there, sir. I—I didn't hear you come in, I guess. Sorry."

"That's all right, Al. I was just standing here listening to you talk. You have a very pungent way of expressing yourself when you instruct newcomers."

Mason smiled uncertainly. "Thank you, sir." He was inwardly tense, wondering just what he had said in the five or ten minutes Henderson might have been standing there. From time to time the C.O. developed a Haroun al-Raschid complex and went wandering about quietly eavesdropping on his subjects. This was evidently one of those times.

But Henderson looked worried. He had that preoccupied frown that could only mean he was getting a hard time from *his* superiors down on Earth.

"Al, could I talk to you privately for a minute?"

"Of course, sir."

They drew away, leaving the apprentices to mutter to each other. Henderson said, "I've just received word from Earthside that the Russians have announced that they're going to telecast from Outpost Kapitza soon."

Mason frowned. *"Really?"*

The C.O. nodded sadly. "Afraid so. Some time in the next two or three months they're going to beam a show all about Kapitza to Earth. Good propaganda, I guess. Unveil the top-secret laboratory, show what they've got hidden away in there. Impress the world with Soviet scientific prowess." Henderson scowled. "Naturally, you know what the Pentagon wants me to do."

"Stage our own telecast, sir?"

"Exactly. Project Me-Too. The merciless eye of the video camera is going to get turned on every dusty corner of Base Three."

Mason's posture sagged wearily. "Heck, sir, what's going to be so fascinating about showing a bunch of test tubes and voltmeters and stuff?"

"I don't know, Al. But we've got to put on the show. That's why I'm making the rounds and talking things over with all the department heads. You've got to start getting your lab shaped up for video."

"And I suppose we'll have to be ready for the cameras next week, so we beat the Russkies."

"Thank goodness, no. We're not doing our show until after the Russians have had theirs. That way, Earthside claims, we'll be able to outdo them. Let them stick their necks out first, in other words." Henderson glanced around. "Will those giant tomatoes be ripe by February?"

"January, sir."

"Delay them till February somehow. Or else get a new batch started that'll be just ripening in February. A couple of shots of tomatoes the size of basketballs is just what we'll need, Al."

"I'll do my best, sir."

"Naturally we'll have to slick the place up a little, too. This is five times as bad as having a few Congressmen come up to inspect. We're having the whole blasted world inspecting us! And I wouldn't want us to come off second best to the Russkies in anything, not even neatness."

Mason nodded.

"One more thing," Henderson went on. "We're planning to give your mechanical cow a big build-up. It's the sort of thing the public will really go for. Yankee ingenuity, all that sort of stuff. Will the new model be in working order by February?"

"I doubt it, sir. You wouldn't want us to rush it along just to make a TV deadline, would you?"

"No, I wouldn't. We'll show the Mark I, then. In fact, that's better than showing the Mark II. The Mark I is so damned complicated-looking, you know—it'll make a big hit with John Q. Public."

"The more complicated it looks, the more scientific he thinks it is. I get you, sir." Mason smiled. "Is there anything else, Commander?"

"Not for now, Al. There'll be regular bulletins as we get this thing shaped up. You'll be asked to submit a sketch of the things you want to be shown in your section. But don't let this nonsense interfere too much with regular work." Henderson made a sour face. "*Propaganda! Pfui!*"

That was just about Mason's own attitude. Lunar Base Three was a research lab, he thought, not a video studio. The thought of cameras poking into one chaotic lab after another irritated and angered him. For the next few months, he knew, nothing would go on at the base but a mass tidying-up campaign to make it look shipshape for the video show. Mason shrugged; Earthside paid the bills, and, he supposed, they were entitled to call the tune. If only the Russkies weren't so propaganda-conscious! And if only we didn't have to play monkey-see monkey-do whenever they made an announcement!

"Okay," Mason hollered to his apprentices. "Let's get back to work!"

For the next half hour he worked them over, only partly resisting the temptation to take out a little resentment on them. He was showing them the algae tanks when the office phone rang. One of the apprentices picked it up.

"It's for you, sir. Doctor Rankin of biology."

Mason grabbed the phone. "Hello, Ned. What's up?"

"The jig, that's what," Rankin said in his hollow voice. "Henderson was just here to tell me about some stupid video show that we're all involved in."

"Yeah, I know. He was here half an hour ago to tell me about it."

"Well, I was down in the lower lab when he came, and he went in there. And he saw Caligula."

"At long last, huh?" Mason laughed. "He must have been surprised."

"Surprised? He almost shot through the dome."

"You mean he was sore?" Mason asked.

"Al, you haven't seen dear little Caligula in a while, have you?"

"No, not for a month or two. Why?"

Rankin said hoarsely, "Al, he's four and a half feet long. I've got him in a tank twelve feet long, and he needs a bigger one."

"Well, what of it? Why was Henderson annoyed?"

"For one thing, because he didn't know anything about the project. He demanded to know where I had gotten an alligator from. He thought it was a crocodile, by the way. I told him I'd requisitioned it a year ago. Played it real innocent, you know. Told him he'd okayed the requisition and everything. He looked at me as though I were crazy. Got on the phone, called up Sam Donohue, and had him read off every requisition on the lists for May, June, and July 1996. So Sam got to the middle of the June list and read off, *'One live baby alligator,'* and claimed the sheet was initialed by Henderson. Al, have you ever seen a man go purple in the face? Henderson did."

"And where did it all end?"

"He took a look at the sheet and admitted he'd signed it —but he doesn't remember okaying any requisitions for alligators."

"Naturally not."

"He claims I must have slipped it through on a busy day, or something."

"Did you explain how successful your experiment is?"

"Yes," Rankin said. "He didn't object to that. He just wanted to know how much bigger Caligula was going to get. He also wants me to file a complete report on the experiment by next Monday."

"Go to it, man!"

"I intend to. But I'm beginning to wish I hadn't ever gotten myself mixed up in this, Al. Something tells me Caligula is going to get a little too big to handle."

Later that evening Mason paid a visit to the bio lab. It was empty; most of the base was at the movies. Mason made his way past the cluttered work-benches into the room where Caligula was kept, and switched on the light.

The alligator's tank was in the center of the room. It was an enormous tank; Mason wondered where and how Rankin had scrounged it. It was ringed with thermometers and other indicating devices of an indescribable variety, each one probably measuring some chemical component of Caligula's water. The alligator himself was perched regally atop a huge lump of lunar rock, basking beneath an ultraviolet lamp. He swivelled one goggly eye around and fixed it on the intruder. The front of his snout still turned up in a grin, but efficient-looking teeth showed around the edges. Caligula had taken on much of the ferocity of his ancient namesake. He bore himself with pride, as he well might, considering that he was some three times the size of every other alligator born in his brood.

Mason picked up a notebook near the tank. Rankin was

recording length measurements. The most recent entry had been taken two hours before; converting out of centimeters, Mason figured it as four feet seven and a half inches. Pretty big for a critter who had been pint-sized only about a year ago. Rankin had succeeded with a vengeance.

It was not until the following Monday, though, that Mason discovered how phenomenal Rankin's success really had been. To be precise, it was 0100 hours on Monday, and Mason was in his quarters getting ready to grab some sleep, when there was a knock at the door and the familiar cavernous voice of Rankin said. "It's me, Al."

"Come on in."

Rankin was carrying a thick portfolio. He sank down limply in a chair, collapsing like a bundle of loose slats, and groaned.

"You look beat," Mason observed.

"I've been working on the report for Henderson all weekend—the report on Caligula. Just finished it. Got it right here. Al, I'm scared green."

"Scared?"

Rankin nodded. "I tabulated all my statistics on Caligula and gave them to one of the math boys to run through the computer. He brought me the results a little while ago." Rankin moistened his lips and drew a yellow sheet from his portfolio. "It seems that Caligula's growth curve is going to increase practically geometrically for a while. If I keep him on the treatment, he's going to grow at a rate of pretty close to nine inches a month for the next six months, and after that at a rate of eleven inches a month until he reaches the length of twenty feet. A size which he will attain, let me add, in approximately another year and a half."

"*Yoik!*"

"Once he's reached twenty feet," Rankin went on, "the growth curve will steadily diminish, until by the time he's forty feet long he'll be growing no faster than an inch a year, or so. It's an asymptotic curve, incidentally. He isn't ever going to stop growing completely for the rest of his natural life. Which, if we coddle him the way we're doing, will be a minimum of a hundred years."

Mason made a gargling sound. "Forty feet—a hundred years—"

"The laboratory I keep him in," Rankin continued, "is exactly twenty-four feet eight inches in length. Obviously it isn't big enough to hold Caligula more than another six months. What's more, by the time he's twenty feet long there won't be *any* lab anyplace in the base where he can be kept and still have room to turn around in."

Mason smiled mirthlessly. "You realized this when you started fooling around with him."

"I figured he'd get to be eight or nine feet long, the way most alligators do. I knew he could theoretically grow forever, but I didn't think my process was as efficient as it turned out to be."

"Well, why don't you take him off that special diet?"

"It doesn't matter," Rankin said mournfully. "His metabolism is already permanently hyped-up. If I cut out the antibiotics and nutrients now, all that would happen would be that he'd slow down a little. It would take him four years to reach twenty feet, instead of a year and a half. But that isn't much consolation. Al, what are we going to do with him?"

Mason shrugged. "As far as I can figure, all we can do is kill him. Slice him into ladies' handbags. Otherwise he'll grow us right out of house and home."

"But I'd hate to kill him, Al. He's so damned majestic. And it would be a dirty trick to put him to death just because he's big."

"We can't keep him here, though. He's going to take up the entire dome if we don't get rid of him. And I'd hate to think of the amount of good meat we're going to have to shovel into that huge body—"

"What are we going to *do,* Al? Can't we save him somehow?"

Mason frowned. "I wish we could, Ned. Maybe we can. Maybe I can think of something. I hope."

Luckily, Base Commander Henderson did not comment on the report Rankin turned in, which meant that he hadn't had time to read it carefully yet. Mason knew there would be yelps of outrage audible all the way to Pluto once Henderson started to read the small print and discovered that a potential dinosaur had been foisted off on him. Caligula's doom would be sealed immediately, if not sooner.

Mason had to admit privately that, once again, his fondness for fun had had grave consequences. Project Bossie too had started off as a gay prank, but in the end they found themselves swiping an entire lab full of equipment for their cow, at a cost of thousands. Which might have gotten Commander Henderson into serious trouble with Congress, had things not gone well.

Here, too, a pleasant jape had boomeranged. It was one thing to oblige a kid researcher by helping him keep his pet alligator; it was another thing entirely when said pet threatens to turn into a monster far beyond the capacity of the base to support. Caligula's gaping jaws already were

31

gulping down a frightening quantity of meat every week—and, since Rankin had done his work all too well, the alligator's appetite would grow in direct proportion to his size, and then some.

For the moment, Commander Henderson was too busy getting that unmentionable telecast arranged to have time to leaf through Rankin's report. The moment he did, though, and came across the projection of Caligula's growth, he was likely to order the immediate cessation of Rankin's experiment and the even more immediate dismemberment of the calibrated alligator. Which would be a pity, Mason thought. Caligula was too noble a creature to deserve so ignominious a fate as conversion into shoes, belts, and handbags.

Sadly, though, Mason admitted that the hopes for Caligula's survival were slim. A lunar dome has only a limited amount of space, and is definitely not designed with forty-foot alligators in mind, or even twenty-foot ones. Of manageable size now, Caligula would soon be awesome, if Rankin's growth curves were right—and, alas, they probably were.

No answer was in sight. After a couple of days of wrestling with possible solutions, Mason let the matter slip from his mind. He had to knuckle down and start preparing his lab for the forthcoming telecast. He could not worry about Caligula.

For the next month progress ground to a halt at Lunar Base Three, while plans for the telecast were being hatched. The problem of Caligula receded.

Then, one night, word came that the Russian telecast was imminent. Video sets were hastily rigged together and mounted in the recreation sheds. The men of Lunar Base Three gathered together to see just what the comrades had to show.

The telecast was in Russian, of course. The Earthside stations that were picking up the signal for transmission to their own audiences would naturally dub in a simultaneous translation in appropriate languages, whether English, French, Turkish, or Swahili. But there was no need for a dubbing job to be done at Lunar Base Three. For the last couple of decades, it had been not only academically required, but sheer common sense as well, for any man planning to do scientific work to acquire a good working knowledge of Russian. That way, you didn't have to hope for a translation to become available, whenever some document vital to your particular specialty was published in a Russian technical journal.

The men of Base Three watched the telecast with a good deal of interest. There was little contact between the American dome and its Marxist counterpart in Ptolemaeus Crater, and nobody knew exactly what the Russians were currently working on in there. But, as it happened, their laboratories looked astonishingly like the American laboratories. The NO SMOKING signs were in Cyrillic instead of Roman characters, but the general appearance of the sections was unremarkable. Nor were the Russians up to anything outré. There was a cryogenics lab, a hydroponics section, a genetics wing, an annex for solid-state work, high- and low-pressure physics lab, atmospherics, nucleonics, gravitics—all the usuals. Of course, nothing of a classified nature was going to be shown; maybe the Russians were running tests on a functional death ray in their dome too, but if they were they would probably choose to keep it to themselves for a while longer. Nor did the straining eyes of the Base Three personnel pick up any useful hints of Soviet procedures that could be appropriated with profit.

It was sheer propaganda for the layman: "Look what an elaborate laboratory we've built here," the Russians were saying. "Look how interested we are in solving the secrets of the universe"—which was all well and good, all perfectly true.

The Russian lab was impressive—though not a whit more so than the American.

One thing that aroused Al Mason's interest was the fact that the Russian presentation was utterly humorless. Not once did a Soviet scientist smile when demonstrating his specialty; nothing of the order of the milk-producing machine was shown, either. All was grim seriousness over in Outpost Kapitza, it seemed.

And then, as an unexpected fillip at the end, the Russians unveiled their bear.

"Here is the mascot of Outpost Kapitza," the Russian commentator declared sonorously, and the cameras focussed on a rotund little bear about three feet high. "The animal is beloved of us all, here. He represents the strength and tenacity of Marxian Socialism. To us, he symbolizes the spirit of Outpost Kapitza. As a bear will cling without fear to its quarry, so, too, do we pursue our goals diligently and unshakeably—to their ultimate attainment. This has been Outpost Kapitza broadcasting. Thank you."

The telecast was over.

The consensus of opinion, radioed up from Washington

the next day, was that the Russians had done a pretty good job of their presentation. It had been serious, for the most part; it had demonstrated what needed no demonstration, the fact that the Soviets were making splendid progress in just about every field of science; and, by showing the little roly-poly bear at the very end of the program, the Russians had wiped out completely the rather impersonal tone of their demonstration, and had left in its place an impression of warm humanity. After all, people who are softhearted enough to keep a furry mascot in their laboratory can't really be *evil*, can they?

The word came from the Pentagon: the American telecast, which was scheduled to follow in three weeks, had better be good, with a capital G. Public relations experts would be coming up in the next ship to help in the preparation of the showing. America's television networks were pooling their talent to send the best directors, cameramen, and scriptwriters. Lunar Base Three's answer to the Soviets would have to be Quite A Show, or heads would roll. The undertones in the directive from Washington were distinctly sinister. To be outdone by the Russians in science might be bad enough; to be outdone in the art of television broadcasting would be a catastrophe.

The public relations experts, directors, cameramen, and writers duly arrived. Lunar Base Three was overrun with them. They were everywhere, jotting down notes, chalking camera angles, talking to technicians, and generally disrupting the normal work of the base.

The day of the telecast drew nearer and nearer. An air of tension hung over the base. Speeches were written, condensed, expanded, scrapped.

And somehow, in the midst of all the confusion and turmoil, Commander Henderson found time finally to leaf through the report Rankin had submitted on his growth-acceleration project.

Al Mason was supervising the uptidying of the hydroponics lab when his phone rang. He snatched it up impatiently.

"Mason here."

"Al, this is Ned Rankin. The explosion has come."

"Huh? What—"

"Henderson! He finally read my report. He called me up two minutes ago and said to me, 'Are you serious when you say that this alligator is going to grow to be forty feet long?' So I said yes, and he started to gargle and choke, and finally he told me to get over to his office on the double and give him an explanation. Heck, Al, what am I supposed to tell him?"

Mason ran his tongue nervously over his lips. "Let me do the talking. Meet me in front of the administration hut and I'll go in there with you."

Commander Henderson's usually uncluttered desk was piled high with memoranda about the forthcoming telecast. But he was holding a familiar-looking portfolio gripped tightly in both hands, and the expression on his face was not a benign one.

It became even more stormy when Mason walked into his office along with Ned Rankin.

"What are *you* doing here, Mason? I asked to see Rankin, not to have the whole damned base in here."

"Well, sir," Rankin began tremulously. "He—"

"I happen to be involved somewhat in this alligator thing, sir," Mason said calmly.

Henderson's eyebrows rose half an inch. "You? Aren't you busy enough with your hydroponics and your cow? Do you have to be mixed up in *every* bit of whackiness that goes on up here? Just how are you involved in this, Mason?"

"I—ah—was responsible for persuading Dr. Rankin to undertake the project. He was a little hesitant, you see, so I prodded him."

"And it's noble of you to step forth and admit that now, I guess," Henderson said icily. He glared upward from the portfolio. "I read in this report of Rankin's that you expect Caligula, or whatever you call him, to reach a length of twenty feet some time in 1998, and that eventually he's going to be forty feet long. Where, may I ask, did you plan to keep a forty-foot alligator? Where would you even keep a *twenty*-foot alligator? Do you do these things *deliberately*, Mason?"

Mason smiled thinly. "He *is* going to be rather large, isn't he, sir?"

"Yes. He is. And one more thing." Henderson transfixed them both with malevolent glares. "I have no recollection of okaying any requisitions for alligators, despite the evidence in the files of the requisitions clerk. I don't remember receiving either a formal or an informal request to carry on this project, either, Rankin. All I knew was that one day it was a *fait accompli*—there was a yard and a half of alligator living in a tank in your lab, and I was supposed to have okayed it some time in the misty past. That made me suspicious. So I went to the rather violent extreme of phoning Earthside and having them check cargo manifests for the entire year of 1996. There wasn't a single reference to the shipping of a single blasted alligator. Now, isn't that odd? Mason, you're probably responsible, so why don't you tell me where that beast came from in the first place? Was he spontaneously generated? Did he stow away on a cargo ship? Did you find him crawling around on the naked face of the moon? Is he a Russian spy? Where did he come from, anyway?"

Mason gulped. A bead of sweat dribbled down his forehead. He thought of cryogenics technician Ross furtively collecting snips of meat for his tiny pet. No point getting Ross in trouble on account of this. He would be leaving the moon at the end of the year anyway, having used up his grant.

In a strained voice Mason said, "Sir, let's be practical about this. The real problem now isn't where the alligator came from, but what we're going to do with him."

Henderson nodded agreeably. "Okay. For the moment, we'll overlook the question of origin. I'm even willing to let it be overlooked permanently. Just tell me what you plan to do with this monster that you and Rankin have been nurturing?"

Rankin said feebly, "Why, the experiment will be terminated, and I guess the alligator will have to be destroyed—"

"*Destroyed?*" Mason shrieked. "Destroy a tangible proof of our accomplishment at Lunar Base Three?" Wheels were turning in his head, suddenly. "We can't destroy Caligula, Rankin. He's our Exhibit A."

Henderson rose to his full height and glared at the hydroponics technician. "Would you mind telling me what you're babbling about, Mason?"

"Certainly, sir. But first—have you read Rankin's report in detail? About the value of the application of his process to herbivorous reptiles, as a new and economical food source?"

"Yes, but—"

"Rankin didn't see fit to go into the details, but it's obvious that the growth acceleration treatment has tremendous value to the people of Earth as well as the inhabitants of the Moon bases. And anything which has food value to Earth has tremendous propaganda value too."

"So?"

"The Russians showed their pet bear, didn't they? Well, on *our* telecast, we can show our alligator. Explain just how old he is, and why he happens to be so big for his age. And what he means to the Moon and to Earth in terms of unlocking an enormous new source of cheap food. It'll be a propaganda coup, sir!"

"But that still doesn't tell me what we're going to do with that monster up here," Commander Henderson objected.

Mason smiled. "Oh, we won't keep him here, sir. He'll be famous after the telecast. We'll send him back to Earth, where everyone can see him. He can be a visible demonstration of the Rankin Process. An alligator on Earth is worth ten on the Moon, sir."

Rankin frowned. "But the cost of shipping—"

"*What* cost?" Mason demanded. "The big budget item is fuel to get stuff from the Earth to here; it isn't more than a tiny fraction as expensive to send things in the other direction. And there's always plenty of room on the cargo ships when they leave for their return leg to Earth. Room enough for Caligula, at any rate."

The Calibrated Alligator

He stopped. The Commander was smiling. After one doubtful moment, Rankin started to smile too, and then all three began to laugh.

Lunar Base Three's telecast was a great success, carried off with the skill and professionalism that all had hoped for. Commander Henderson himself narrated it. Cameras were set up all over the base, and the scene shifted rapidly from one laboratory to the other, with each department head explaining briefly and within security limitations what he was working on. Commander Henderson provided a commentary to bridge each separate talk, and he handled himself ably.

A high-point of the screening was the visit to Room 106a, which contained Project Bossie. Al Mason discussed in some considerable detail how the milk-synthesizer functioned and capped the demonstration by gulping a pint of Bossie-produced milk with evident delight.

And finally, after each of the research wings of Lunar Base Three had had its televised moment of glory, the cameras shifted to a room in the biology laboratory. All extraneous calibrating equipment had been cleared away from Caligula's tank, leaving the alligator—now a full five feet in length—exposed to full view.

As Caligula peered majestically into the lens of the camera, Commander Henderson's voice delivered a sonorous peroration.

"We come now to the conclusion of our tour of Lunar Base Three. And on your screen now is *our* mascot—Caligula. Born in Florida's Everglades, he has spent his entire adult life in Lunar Base Three, floating here in proud majesty. Not a man of our staff fails to admire Caligula's lofty bearing and regal poise. To us, he represents a link with the past ages of Earth's history. Unchanged over millions of years, the alligator has come down to us out of the dim mists of the Mesozoic. Here on the Moon, he serves to remind us of how short a span of time the era of man has actually covered—not even a visible fraction of the eons that alligators have inhabited the Earth. And yet, in our few centuries of existence, we have dared to fling our gauntlet outward, to the stars. Who knows what mankind will accomplish by the time our race is as old as Caligula's now is?"

The Commander paused. Then, descending from the flowery heights of oratory, he added in a less resounding tone, "But Caligula is not only a pet here. He is an experimental animal as well—and the experiment he has taken part in will have incalculable benefit for you, the people of the Earth."

The camera panned to Ned Rankin, who was standing behind Caligula's tank.

Commander Henderson said, "Here is Dr. Rankin of our biology staff, who will explain Caligula's importance to humanity."

Ned Rankin grinned good-naturedly and said, "Caligula, you see, is the prototype for a new breed of reptile—a reptile that grows to great size in a short period of time. Not much more than a year ago, Caligula was just a ten-inch alligatorlet." He indicated the size with his hands. "If left to develop normally, he'd be about a foot and a half long, now. Instead, he's reached a length of five feet, and will continue growing until he is of truly enormous size— perhaps as much as forty feet.

"This phenomenal growth has been achieved through special techniques developed at Lunar Base Three. You

41

may wonder, what is so important about having grown a huge alligator?" Rankin smiled. "The importance, ladies and gentlemen of Earth, is that this process can be applied to reptiles such as the iguana, whose meat is considered a delicacy nowadays. An enormous new supply of food— meat—is now available to mankind.

"It'll be a few years, of course, before the first iguana meat reaches your dinner table. But this particular development of Lunar Base Three will help to insure that there will be no more of the meatless Tuesdays that you have had to endure lately. Growing faster than cattle, requiring far less care, just as nutritious—you see the multiplicity of advantages that this new development will have. An Earth confronted with a critical shortage of meat has been reprieved. The great problem of the century to come has been alleviated."

The camera took in Caligula once again. Commander Henderson spoke again. "Thank you, Ned Rankin, for your explanation—and the whole world thanks you for the process you have developed. And, ladies and gentlemen, I'd like to add here that very soon you will be able to view Caligula with your own eyes. Yes, we have decided to send him to Earth. By special arrangements just concluded before we took the air, Caligula will be shipped to Earth for exhibition at the major zoological gardens of the world. We'll miss him here, but we send him to you as visible proof of our work here. And as he grows to giant size, he'll serve as a reminder that the men of Lunar Base Three never cease in their endeavor to improve the welfare of humanity.

"Thank you, and good night from Lunar Base Three."

The telecast, having been relayed by orbital pickups

42

round the world, had been viewed by an estimated two billion people. And the reverberations from Washington the next day were loud and approving.

In Commander Henderson's office, the commander said to Al Mason and Ned Rankin, "The wire is flooded with congratulations on our telecast. There's talk in Congress of doubling our appropriation. Everybody's buzzing about Caligula, and the zoos are squabbling like crazy for the right to be the first to show him."

"They'd better have a big tank ready," Mason said. "And plenty of raw meat."

"The iguana business really has them all standing on their heads, though," the commander went on. "The government was planning to announce tougher meat rationing next year, and they were worried about the effect it would have on the elections. But now they're cancelling the new restrictions, pending the introduction of iguana farming. You'd better get started on a full and detailed report, Ned. They're ready to get into iguana production down there the moment you give the word."

"We'll need some up here, too," Rankin said. "My computations show that six pairs of iguanas, if treated with my process, will grow and reproduce fast enough so that after six months they'll be producing enough meat to supply the entire base twice a week—which means a good many tons of scientific equipment that can be shipped up here each month instead of that execrable synthetic meat. And the iguana supply is not only self-replenishing but will require a minimum of food and care in return for a maximum of edible meat."

"Not to mention the important factor of introducing some variety into our diet," Mason added.

"The ship is leaving next week," Henderson said. "With Caligula on board. And it'll bring your iguanas on the return trip."

"Poor old Caligula," Rankin said. "I'm going to miss him, I'm afraid."

"We just aren't set up for raising monsters up here, Ned," said Mason. "Another few years and we would have had to build a special dome just for him. Down on Earth, he can grow to forty or fifty feet in peace—and every yard he grows is another feather in our cap."

Commander Henderson nodded. "It's a great achievement all around. And you've pulled a silk purse out of a sow's ear again, eh, Mason? Last time a source of milk—now cheap meat, not to mention a propaganda coup that completely obliterated the impact of the Russian telecast."

"It wasn't my doing, sir. Rankin invented the process. I simply aided in a minor sort of way."

"That isn't true, sir!" Rankin blurted. "If it weren't for Mason, we would never—"

Mason kicked him sharply. Rankin shrugged and shut up. Commander Henderson fixed them both with a steely gaze. "There's just one thing bothering me about this whole project," he said. "I've been meaning to ask you: if the point of it was to accelerate the growth of herbivorous reptiles, how come you started with an *alligator?*"

"Well, sir," Rankin began, "we happened to have—"

Mason kicked him again, harder. "It's sort of complicated, sir," he said quickly. "It's a long story that isn't really worth the time it would take to tell it."

Commander Henderson sighed. "The translation being that you were up to something you shouldn't have been up

44

to. Oh, well, Mason. I know when I'm licked. I won't push you any harder on the subject of where that alligator came from in the first place. It doesn't really matter, now. Not in view of the results." He picked up a piece of paper. "I just wish I had some way of knowing what you'll be up to next," he said wistfully. "No, cancel that. Life would be a lot duller up here if I did."

Blaze of Glory

They list John Murchison as one of the great heroes of space—a brave man and true, who willingly sacrificed himself to save his ship. He won his immortality on the way back from Shaula II.

One thing's wrong, though. He was brave, but he wasn't willing. He wasn't the self-sacrificing type. I'm inclined to think it was murder, or maybe execution. By remote control, you might say.

I guess they pick spaceship crews at random—say, by yanking a handful of cards from the big computer and throwing them up at the BuSpace roof. The ones that stick get picked. At least, that's the only way a man like Murchison could have been sent to Shaula II in the first place.

He was a spaceman of the old school, tall, bullnecked, coarse-featured, hard-swearing. He was a spaceman of a type that had never existed except in storytapes for the very young—the only kind Murchison was likely to have viewed. He was our chief signal officer.

Somewhere, he had picked up an awesome technical competence; he could handle any sort of communication device with supernatural ease. I once saw him tinker with a complex little Caphian artifact that had been buried for half a million years, and have it detecting the 21-centimeter "hydrogen song" within minutes. How he knew the little widget was a star-mapping device I will never understand.

But coupled with Murchison's extraordinary special skill was an irascibility, a self-centered inner moodiness flaring into seemingly unmotivated anger at unpredictable times, that made him a prime risk on a planet like Shaula II. There was something wrong with his circuit-breaker setup: you could never tell when he'd overload, start fizzing and sparking, and blow off a couple of megawatts of temper.

You must admit this is not the ideal sort of man to send to a world whose inhabitants are listed in the E-T Catalogue as *"wise, somewhat world-weary, exceedingly gentle, non-aggressive to an extreme degree and thus subject to exploitation. The Shaulans must be handled with great patience and forbearance, and should be given the respect due one of the galaxy's elder races."*

I had never been to Shaula II, but I had a sharp mental image of the Shaulans: melancholy old men pondering the whichness of the why and ready to fall apart at the first loud voice that caught them by surprise. So it caught *me* by surprise when the time came to affix my hancock to the roster of the *Felicific,* and I saw on the line above mine the scribbled words *Murchison, John F., Signalman First Class.*

I signed my name—*Loeb, Ernest T., Second Officer*—picked up my pay voucher, and walked away somewhat dizzily. I was thinking of the time I had seen Murchison,

John F., giving a Denebolan frogman the beating of his life, for no particular reason at all. "All the rain here makes me sick" was all Murchison cared to say; the frogman lived and Big Jawn got an X on his psych report.

Now he was shipping out for Shaula? Well, maybe so . . . but my faith in the computer that makes up spaceship complements was seriously shaken.

We were the fourth or fifth expedition to Shaula II. The planet—second of seven in orbit round the brightest star in Scorpio's tail—was small and scrubby, but of great strategic importance as a lookout spot for that sector of the galaxy. The natives hadn't minded our intrusion, and so a military base had been established there after a little preliminary haggling.

The *Felicific* was a standard warp-conversion-drive ship holding thirty-six men. It had the usual crew of eight, plus a cargo of twenty-eight of Terra's finest, being sent out as replacements for the current staff of the base.

We blasted on 3 July 2530, a warmish day, made the conversion from ion-drive to warp-drive as soon as we were clear of the local system, and popped back into normal space three weeks later and two hundred light-years away. It was a routine trip in all respects.

With the warp-conversion drive, a ship is equipped to travel both long distances and short. It handles the long hops via subspace warp, and the short ones by good old standard ion-drive seat-of-the-spacesuit navigating. It's a good system, and the extra mass the double drive requires is more than compensated for by the saving in time and maneuverability.

48

Blaze of Glory

The warp-drive part of the trip was pre-plotted and just about pre-traveled for us; no headaches *there*. But when we blurped back into the continuum about half a light-year from Shaula the human factor entered the situation. Meaning Murchison, of course.

It was his job to check and tend the network of tele-metering systems that acted as the ship's eyes, to make sure the mass-detectors were operating, to smooth the bugs out of the communications channels between navigator and captain and drive-deck. In brief, he was the man who made it possible for us to land.

Every ship carried a spare signalman, just in case. In normal circumstances the spare never got much work. When the time came for the landing, Captain Knight buzzed me and told me to start lining up the men who would take part, and I signalled Murchison first.

His voice was a slow rasping drawl. "Yeah?"

"Second Officer Loeb. Prepare for landing, double-fast. Navigator Henrichs has the chart set up for you and he's waiting for your call."

There was a pause. Then: "I don't feel like it, Loeb."

It was my turn to pause. I shut my eyes, held my breath, and counted to three by fractions. Then I said, "Would you mind repeating that, Signalman Murchison?"

"Yes, sir. No, sir, I mean. Hell, Loeb, I'm fixing some-thing. Why do you want to land now?"

"I don't make up the schedules," I said.

"Then who in blazes does? Tell him I'm busy!"

I turned down my phones' volume. "Busy doing what?"

"Busy doing nothing. Get off the line and I'll call Hen-richs."

I sighed and broke contact. He'd just been ragging me. Once again, Murchison had been ornery for the sheer sake of being ornery. One of these days he was going to refuse to handle the landing entirely.

And that day, I told myself, is the day we'll crate him up and shove him through the disposal lock.

Murchison was a little island. He had his skills, and he applied them—when he felt like it. But only when he believed that he, Murchison, would profit. He never did anything unwillingly, because if he couldn't find it in himself to do it willingly he wouldn't do it at all. It was impossible to *make* him do something.

Unwisely, we tolerated it. But someday he would get a captain who didn't understand him, and he'd be slapped with a sentence of mutiny during a fit of temperament. For his sake, I hoped not. The penalty for mutiny in space is death.

With Murchison's cooperation gratefully accepted, we targeted on Shaula II, which was then at perihelion, and orbited it. Down in his little cubicle Murchison worked like a demon, taking charge of the ship's landing system in a tremendous way. He was a fantastic signalman when he wanted to be.

Later that day the spinning red ball that was Shaula II hung just ahead of us, close enough to let us see the three blobs of continents and the big, choppy hydrocarbon ocean that licked them smooth. The Terran base on Continent Three beamed us a landing-guide; Murchison picked it up, fed it through the computer bank to Navigator Henrichs, and we homed in for the landing.

Blaze of Glory

The Terran base consisted of a couple of blockhouses, a sprawling barracks, and a good-sized radar parabola, all set in a ring out on an almost mathematically flat plain. Shaula II was a great world for plains; Columbus would have had the devil's time convincing people *this* world was round!

Murchison guided us to a glassy-looking area not far from the base, and we touched down. The *Felicific* creaked and groaned a little as the landing-jacks absorbed its weight. Green lights went on all over the ship. We were free to go outside.

A welcoming committee was on hand: eight members of the base staff, clad in shorts and topees. Regulation uniforms went by the board on oven-hot Shaula II. The eight looked awfully happy to see us.

Coming over the flat sandy plain from the base were a dozen or so others, running, and behind them I could see even more. They were understandably glad we were here. Twenty-eight of them had spent a full year on Shaula II; they were eligible for their parity-program year's vacation.

There were some other—things—moving toward us. They moved slowly, with grace and dignity. I had expected to be impressed with the Shaulans, and I was.

They were erect bipeds about four feet tall, with long thin arms dangling to their knees; their gray skins were grainy and rough, and their dark eyes—they had three, arranged triangularly—were deepset and brooding. A fleshy sort of cowl or cobra-hood curled up from their necks to shield their round hairless skulls. The aliens were six in number, and the youngest-looking of them seemed ancient.

A brown-faced young man wearing shorts, topee, and

51

tattooed stars stepped forward and said, "I'm General Gloster. I'm in charge here."

The Captain acknowledged his greeting. "Knight of the *Felicific*. We have your relief men with us."

"I sure as hell hope you do," Gloster said. "Be kind of silly to come all this way without them."

We all laughed a little over that. By now we were ringed in by at least fifty Earthmen, probably the entire base complement (we didn't rotate the entire base staff at once, of course), and the six aliens. The twenty-eight kids we had ferried here were looking around the place curiously, apprehensive about this hot, dry, flat planet that would be their home for the next sidereal year. The crew of the *Felicific* had gathered in a little knot near the ship. Most of them probably felt the way I did; they were glad we'd be on our way home in a couple of days.

Murchison was squinting at the six aliens. I wondered what he was thinking about.

The bunch of us traipsed back the half mile or so to the settlement; Gloster walked with Knight and myself, prattling volubly about the progress the base was making, and the twenty-eight newcomers mingled with the twenty-eight who were being relieved. Murchison walked by himself, kicking up puffs of red dust and scowling in his usual manner. The six aliens accompanied us at some distance.

"We keep building all the time," Gloster explained when we were within the compound. "Branching out, setting up new equipment, shoring up the old stuff. That radar parabola out there wasn't up, last replacement-trip."

I looked around. "The place looks fine, General." It was strange calling a man half my age *General,* but the Service sometimes works that way. "When do you plan to set up your telescope?"

"Next year, maybe." He glanced out the window at the featureless landscape. "We keep building all the time. It's the best way to stay sane on this world."

"How about the natives?" the Captain asked. "You have much contact with them?"

Gloster shrugged. "As much as they'll allow. They're a proud old race—pretty near dried up and dead now, just a handful of them left. But what a race they must have been once! What minds! What culture!"

I found Gloster's boyish enthusiasm discomforting. "Do you think we could meet one of the aliens before we go?" I asked.

"I'll see about it." Gloster picked up a phone. "McHenry? There any natives in the compound now? Good. Send him up, will you?"

Moments later one of the shorts-clad men appeared, hand in hand with an alien. At close range the Shaulan looked almost frighteningly old. A maze of wrinkles gullied its noseless face, running from the triple optics down to the dots of nostrils to the sagging, heavy-lipped mouth.

"This is Azga," Gloster said. "Azga, meet Captain Knight and Second Officer Loeb, of the *Felicific*."

The creature offered a wobbly sort of curtsey and said, in a deep, resonant, almost-human croak, "I am very humble indeed in your presence, Captain Knight and Second Officer Loeb."

Azga came out of the curtsey and the three eyes fixed on mine. I felt like squirming, but I stared back. It was like looking into a mirror that gave the wrong reflection.

Yet I enjoyed my proximity to the alien. There was something calm and wise and good about the grotesque creature; something relaxing, and terribly fragile. The rough gray skin looked like precious leather, and the hood over the skull appeared to shield it from worry and harm. A faint musty odor wandered through the room.

We looked at each other—Knight, and Gloster, and McHenry, and I—and we remained silent. Now that the Shaulan was here, what could we say? What *new* thing could we possibly tell the ancient creature?

I resisted an impulse to kneel. I was fumbling for words to express my emotion when the sharp buzz of the phone cut across the room.

Gloster nodded curtly to McHenry, who answered. The man listened for a moment. "Captain Knight, it's for you."

Puzzled, Knight took the receiver. He held it long enough to hear about three sentences and turned to me. "Loeb, get a landcar from someone in the compound and get back to the ship. Murchison's carrying on with one of the aliens."

I hotfooted down into the compound and spotted an enlisted man tooling up his landcar. I pulled rank and requisitioned it, and minutes later I was parking it outside the *Felicific* and was clambering hand-over-hand up the catwalk.

An excited-looking recruit stood at the open airlock.

"Where's Murchison?" I asked.

"Down in the communicator cabin. He's got an alien in there with him. There's gonna be trouble."

I remembered Denebola, and Murchison kicking the stuffings out of a groaning frogman. I groaned a little myself, and dashed down the companionway.

Blaze of Glory

The communications cabin was Murchison's *sanctum sanctorum,* a cubicle off the astro deck where he worked and kept control over the *Felicific's* communications network. I yanked open the door and saw Murchison at the far end of the cabin holding a massive crescent wrench and glaring at a Shaulan facing him. The Shaulan had its back to me. It looked small and squat and helpless.

Murchison saw me as I entered. "Get out of here, Loeb. This isn't your affair."

"What's going on here?" I snapped.

"This alien snooping around. I'm gonna let him have it with the wrench."

"I meant no harm," the alien boomed sadly. "Mere philosophical interest in your strange machines, nothing more. If I have offended a folkway of yours I humbly apologize. It is not the way of my people to give offense."

I walked forward and took a position between them, making sure I wasn't within easy reach of Murchison's wrench. He was standing there with his nostrils spread, his eyes cold and hard, his breath pumping noisily. He was angry, and an angry Murchison was a frightening sight.

He took two heavy steps toward me. "I told you to get out. This is my cabin, Loeb. And neither you or any aliens got any business in it."

"Put down that wrench, Murchison. It's an order."

He laughed contemptuously. "Signalman First Class don't have to take orders from anyone but the Captain if he thinks the safety of the ship is jeopardized. And I do. There's a dangerous alien in here."

"Be reasonable," I said. "This Shaulan's not dangerous. He just wanted to look around. Just curious."

The wrench wiggled warningly. I wished I had a blaster

with me, but I hadn't thought of bringing a weapon. The alien faced Murchison quite complacently, as if confident the signalman would never strike anything so old and delicate.

"You'd better leave," I said to the alien.

"No!" Murchison roared. He shoved me to one side and went after the Shaulan.

The alien stood there, waiting, as Murchison came on. I tried to drag the big man away, but there was no stopping him.

At least he didn't use the wrench. He let the big crescent slip clangingly to the floor and slapped the alien open-handed across its face. The Shaulan backed up a few feet. A trickle of bluish fluid worked its way along its mouth. Murchison raised his hand again. "Damned snooper! I'll teach you to poke in my cabin!" He hit the alien again.

This time the Shaulan folded up accordionwise and huddled on the floor. It focussed those three deep solid-black eyes on Murchison reproachfully.

Murchison looked back. They stared at each other for a long moment, until it seemed that their eyes were linked by an invisible cord. Then Murchison looked away.

"Get out of here," he muttered to the alien, and the Shaulan rose and departed, limping a little but still intact. Those aliens were more solid than they seemed.

"I guess you're going to put me in the brig," Murchison said to me. "Okay. I'll go quietly."

We didn't brig him, because there was nothing to be gained by that. I had seen the explosion coming right from the start. When you drop a lighted match into a tub of hydrazine, you don't punish the hydrazine for blowing up. And Murchison couldn't be blamed for what he did, either.

He got the silent treatment instead. The men at the base would have nothing to do with him whatsoever, because in their year on Shaula they had developed a respect for the aliens not far from worship, and any man who would actually use physical violence—well, he just wasn't worth wasting breath on.

The men of our crew gave him a wide berth too. He wandered among us, a tall, powerful figure with anger and loneliness stamped on his face, and he said nothing to any of us and no one said anything to him. Whenever he saw one of the aliens, he went far out of his way to avoid a meeting.

Murchison got another X on his psych report, and that second X meant he'd never be allowed to visit any world inhabited by intelligent life again. It was a BuSpace regulation, one of the many they have for the purpose of locking the barn door too late.

Three days went by this way on Shaula. On the fourth, we took aboard the twenty-eight departing men, said goodbye to Gloster and his staff and the twenty-eight we had ferried out to him, and—somewhat guiltily—goodbye to the Shaulans too.

The six of them showed up for our blastoff, including the somewhat battered one who had had the run-in with Murchison. They wished us well, gravely, without any sign of bitterness. For the hundredth time I was astonished by their patience, their wisdom, their understanding.

I held Azga's rough hand in mine and said goodbye. I told him for the first time what I had been wanting to say since our first meeting, how much I hoped we'd eventually reach the mental equilibrium and inner calm of the Shaulans. He smiled warmly at me, and I said goodbye again and entered the ship.

We ran the usual pre-blast checkups, and got ready for departure. Everything was working well; Murchison had none of his usual grumbles and complaints, and we were off the ground in record time.

A couple of days of ion-drive, three weeks of warp, two more of ion-drive deceleration, and we would be back on Earth.

The three weeks passed slowly, of course; when Earth lies ahead of you, time drags. But after the interminable grayness of warp came the sudden wrenching twist and the bright slippery *sliding* feeling as our Bohling generator threw us back into ordinary space.

I pushed down the communicator stud near my arm and heard the voice of Navigator Henrichs saying, "Murchison, give me the coordinates, will you?"

"Hold on," came Murchison's growl. "Patience, Sam. You'll get your coordinates as soon as I got 'em."

There was a pause; then Captain Knight said, "Murchison, what's holding up those coordinates? Where are we, anyway? Turn on the visiplates!"

"*Please*, Captain." Murchison's heavy voice was surprisingly polite. Then he ruined it. "Please, be good enough to shut up and let a man think."

"Murchison—" Knight sputtered, and stopped. We all knew one solid fact about our signalman: he did as he pleased. No one but no one coerced him into anything.

So we waited, spinning end-over-end somewhere in the vicinity of Earth, completely blind behind our wall of metal. Until Murchison chose to feed us some data, we had no way of bringing the ship down.

Three more minutes went by; then the private circuit Knight uses when he wants to talk to me alone lit up, and he said, "Loeb, go down to Communications and see what's holding Murchison up. We can't stay here forever."

"Yessir."

I pocketed a blaster—I hate making mistakes more than once—and left my cabin. I walked numbly to the companionway, turned to the left, hit the drophatch and found myself outside Murchison's door.

I knocked.

"Get away from here, Loeb!" Murchison bellowed from within.

I had forgotten that he had rigged a one-way vision circuit outside his door. I said, "Let me in, Murchison. Let me in or I'll come in blasting."

I heard a heavy sigh. "Come on in, then."

Nervously I pushed the door open and poked my head and the blaster snout in, half expecting Murchison to leap on me from above. But he was sitting at an equipment-jammed desk scribbling notes, which surprised me. I stood waiting for him to look up.

And finally he did. I gasped when I saw his face: drawn, harried, pale, tense. I had never seen an expression like that on Murchison's face before.

"What's going on?" I asked softly. "We're all waiting to get moving, and—"

He turned to face me squarely. "You want to know

what's going on, Loeb? Well, listen: the ship's blind. None of the equipment is reading anything. No telemeter pickup, no visual, no nothing. *You* scrape up some coordinates, if you can."

We held a little meeting half an hour later, in the ship's Common Room. Murchison was there, and Knight, and myself, and Navigator Henrichs, and three representatives of the cargo.

"How did this happen?" Knight demanded.

Murchison shrugged. "It happened while we were in warp. We passed through something—magnetic field, maybe—and bollixed every instrument we have."

Knight glanced at Henrichs. "You ever hear of such a thing happening before?" He seemed to suspect Murchison of funny business.

But Henrichs shook his head. "No, Chief. And there's a good reason why, too. If this happens to a ship, the ship doesn't get back to tell about it."

He was right. With no contact at all with the outside, no information on location or orbits, there was no way to land the ship. And the radio, of course, was dead too; we couldn't even call for help.

Captain Knight looked gray-faced and very old. He asked worriedly, "What could have caused this thing?"

"No one knows what subspace conditions are like," Henrichs said. "It may have been a fluke magnetic field, as Murchison suggests. Or anything at all—an alien entity that swallowed our antennae, for all we know. The question's not what did it, Captain—it's how do we get back."

"Good point. Murchison, is there any chance you can repair the instruments?"

"No."

"Just like that—flat *no?* Hell, man, we've seen you do wonders with instruments on the blink before."

"*No,*" Murchison repeated stolidly. "I tried. I can't do a damned thing."

"That means we're finished, doesn't it?" asked Ramirez, one of our returnees. His voice was a little wild. "We might just as well have stayed on Shaula! At least we'd still be alive!"

"It looks pretty lousy," Henrichs admitted. The thin-faced navigator was frowning blackly. "We don't dare try a blind landing. There's nothing we can do. Nothing at all."

"There's *one* thing," Murchison said.

All eyes turned to him. "What?" Knight asked.

"Put a man in a spacesuit and anchor him to the skin of the ship. Have him guide us in by verbal instructions. It's a way, anyway."

"Pretty farfetched," Henrichs commented.

"Yes, dammit, but it's our only hope!" Murchison snapped. "Stick a man up there and let him talk us in."

"He'd incinerate once we hit Earth's atmosphere," I said. "We'd lose a man and still have to land blind."

Murchison puckered his thick lower lip. "You'll be able to judge the ship's height by hull temperature once you're that close. Besides, once the ship's inside the ionosphere you can use ordinary radio for the rest of the way down. The trick is to get *that* far."

"I think it's worth a try," Captain Knight said. "I guess we'll have to draw lots. Loeb, get some straws from the galley." His voice was grim.

"Never mind," Murchison said.

"Huh?"

"I said, never mind. Skip it. Forget about drawing straws. *I'll* go."

"Murchison—"

"*Skip it!*" he barked. "It's a failure in my department, so I'm going to go out there. I volunteer, get it? If anyone else wants to volunteer, I'll match him for it." He looked around at us. No one moved. "I don't hear any takers. I'll assume the job's mine." Sweat streamed down his face.

There was a startled silence, broken when Ramirez made the lousiest remark I've ever heard mortal man utter. "You're trying to make it up for hitting that defenseless Shaulan, eh, Murchison? Now you want to be a hero to even things up!"

If Murchison had killed him on the spot, I think we'd all have applauded. But the big man only turned to Ramirez and said quietly, "You're just as blind as the others. You don't know how rotten those defenseless Shaulans are, any of you. Or what they did to me." He spat. "You all make me sick. I'm going out there."

He turned and walked away . . . out, to get into his space-suit and climb onto the ship's skin.

Murchison's explicit instructions, relayed from the outside of the ship, allowed Henrichs to bring us in. It was quite a feat of teamwork.

At 50,000 feet above Earth, Murchison's voice suddenly cut out. We were able to pick up ground-to-ship radio by then and we taxied down. Later, they told us it seemed like a blazing candle was riding the ship's back. A bright, clear flame flared for a moment as we cleaved the atmosphere.

And I remember the look on Murchison's face as he left us to go out there. It was tense, bitter, strained—as if he were being *compelled* to go outside. As if he had no choice about volunteering for martyrdom.

I often wonder about that now. No one had ever made Murchison do anything he didn't want to do—until then.

We think of the Shaulans as gentle, meek, defenseless. Murchison crossed one of them, and he died. Gentle, meek, yes—but defenseless? Murchison didn't think so.

Maybe they whammied the ship and cursed Murchison with the urge to self-martyrdom, to punish him. Maybe. He never did trust them much.

It sort of tarnishes his glorious halo. But you know, sometimes I think Murchison was right about the Shaulans after all.

The Artifact Business

The Voltuscian was a small, withered humanoid whose crimson throat-appendages quivered nervously, as if the thought of doing archaeological fieldwork excited him unbearably. He gestured to me anxiously with one of his four crooked arms, urging me onward over the level silt.

"This way, friend. Over here is the Emperor's grave."

"I'm coming, Dolbak." I trudged forward, feeling the weight of the spade and the knapsack over my shoulder. I caught up with him a few moments later.

He was standing near a rounded hump in the ground, pointing downward. "This is it," he said happily. "I have saved it for you."

I fished in my pocket, pulled out a tinkling heap of arrow-shaped coins, and handed him one. The Voltuscian, nodding his thanks effusively, ran around behind me to help me unload.

Taking the spade from him, I thrust it into the ground

and began to dig. The thrill of discovery started to tingle in me, as it does always when I begin a new excavation. I suppose that is the archaeologist's greatest joy, that moment of apprehension as the spade first bites into the ground. I dug rapidly and smoothly, following Dolbak's guidance.

"There it is," he said reverently. "And a beauty it is, too. Oh, Jarrell-sir, how happy I am for you!"

I leaned on my spade to recover my wind before bending to look. I mopped away beads of perspiration, and thought of the great Schliemann laboring in the stifling heat of Hissarlik to uncover the ruins of Troy. Schliemann has long been one of my heroes—along with the other archaeologists who did the pioneer work in the fertile soil of Mother Earth.

Wearily, I stooped to one knee and fumbled in the fine sand of the Voltuscian plain, groping for the bright object that lay revealed. I worked it loose from its covering of silt and studied it.

"Amulet," I said after a while. "Third Period; unspecified protective charm. Studded with emerald-cut gobrovirs of the finest water." The analysis complete, I turned to Dolbak and grasped his hand warmly. "How can I thank you, Dolbak?"

He shrugged. "Not necessary." Glancing at the amulet, he said, "It will fetch a high price. Some woman of Earth will wear it proudly."

"Ah—yes," I said, a trifle bitterly. Dolbak had touched on the source of my deep frustration and sorrow.

This perversion of archaeology into a source for trinkets and bits of frippery to adorn rich men's homes and wives had always rankled me. Although I have never seen Earth,

The Artifact Business

I like to believe I work in the great tradition of Schliemann and Evans, whose greatest finds were to be seen in the galleries of the British Museum and the Ashmolean, not dangling on the painted bosom of some too-rich wench who has succumbed to the current passion for antiquity.

When the Revival came, when everyone's interest suddenly turned on the ancient world and the treasures that lay in the ground, I felt deep satisfaction—my chosen profession, I thought, now was one that had value to society as well as private worth. How wrong I was! I took this job in the hope that it would provide me with the needed cash to bring me to Earth—but instead I became nothing more than the hired lackey of a dealer in women's fashions, and Earth's unreachable museums lie inch-deep in dust.

I sighed and returned my attention to the excavation. The amulet lay there, flawless in its perfection, a marvelous relic of the great race that once inhabited Voltus. Masking my sadness, I reached down with both hands and lovingly plucked the amulet from the grave in which it had rested so many thousands of years.

I felt a sudden impulse to tip Dolbak again. The withered alien accepted the coins gratefully, but with a certain reserve that made me feel that perhaps this whole business seemed as sordid to him as it did to me.

"It's been a good day's work," I told him. "Let's go back, now. We'll get this assayed and I'll give you your commission, eh, old fellow?"

"That will be very good, sir," he said mildly, and assisted me in donning my gear once again.

We crossed the plain and entered the Terran outpost in silence. As we made our way through the winding streets to the assay office, hordes of the four-armed, purple-hued Voltuscian children approached us clamorously, offering us things for sale, things they had made themselves. Some of their work was quite lovely; the Voltuscians seem to have a remarkable aptitude for handicrafting. But I brushed them all away. I have made it a rule to ignore them, no matter how delightful a spun-glass fingerbowl they may have, how airy and delicate an ivory carving. Such things, being contemporary, have no market value on Earth, and a man of my limited means must avoid luxuries of this sort.

The assay office was still open, and, as we approached, I saw two or three men standing outside, each with his Voltuscian guide.

"Hello, Jarrell," said a tall man raucously.

I winced. He was David Sturges, one of the least scrupulous of the many Company archaeologists on Voltus—a man who thought nothing of breaking into the most sacred shrines of the planet and committing irreparable damage for the sake of ripping loose a single marketable item.

"Hello, Sturges," I said shortly.

"Have a good day, old man? Find anything worth poisoning you for?"

I grinned feebly and nodded. "Nice amulet of the Third Period. I'm planning on handing it in immediately, but if you prefer I won't. I'll take it home and leave it on my table tonight. That way you won't wreck the place looking for it."

"Oh, that won't be necessary," Sturges said. "I came up with a neat cache of enamelled skulls today—a dozen, of the Expansion Era, set with platinum scrollwork." He pointed to his alien guide, a dour-looking Voltuscian named

Qabur. "My boy found them for me. Wonderful fellow, Qabur. He can home in on a cache as if he's got radar in his nose."

I began to frame a reply in praise of my own guide when Zweig, the assayer, stepped to the front of his office and looked out. "Well, who's next? You, Jarrell?"

"Yes, sir." I picked up my spade and followed him inside. He slouched behind his desk and looked up wearily.

"What do you have to report, Jarrell?"

I drew the amulet out of my knapsack and handed it across the desk. He examined it studiously, noticing the way the light glinted off the facets of the inset gobrovirs. "Not bad," he said.

"It's a rather fine piece, isn't it?"

"Not bad," he repeated. "Seventy-five dollars, I'd say."

"*What?* I'd figured that piece for at least five hundred! Come on, Zweig, be reasonable. Look at the quality of those gobrovirs!"

"Very nice," he admitted. "But you have to understand that the gobrovir, while attractive, is intrinsically not a very valuable gem. And I must consider the intrinsic value as well as the historical, you know."

I frowned. Now would come the long speech about supply and demand, the scarcity of gems, the cost of shipping the amulet back to Earth, marketing, on and on, on and on. I spoke before he had the chance. "I won't haggle, Zweig. Give me a hundred and fifty or I'll keep the thing myself."

He grinned slyly. "What would *you* do with it? Donate it to the British Museum?"

The remark stung. I looked at him sadly, and he said, "I'll give you a hundred."

"Hundred and fifty or I keep."

He reached down and scooped ten ten-dollar pieces from a drawer. He spread them out along his desk. "There's the offer," he said. "It's the best the Company can do."

I stared at him for an agonized moment, scowled, took the ten tens, and handed over the amulet. "Here. You can give me thirty pieces of silver for the next one I bring in."

"Don't make it hard for me, Jarrell. This is only my job."

I threw one of the tens to the waiting Dolbak, nodded curtly, and walked out.

I returned to my meager dwelling on the outskirts of the Terran colony in a state of deep dejection. Each time I handed an artifact over to Zweig—and, in the course of the eighteen months since I had accepted this accursed job, I had handed over quite a few—I felt, indeed, a Judas. When I thought of the long row of glass cases my discoveries might have filled, in, say, the Voltus Room of the British, I ached. The crystal shields with double handgrips; the tooth-wedges of finest obsidian; the sculptured ear-binders with their unbelievable filigree of sprockets—these were products of one of the most fertile creative civilizations of all, the Old Voltuscians—and these treasures were being scattered to the corners of the galaxy as trinkets.

The amulet today—what had I done with it? Turned it over to—to a *procurer,* virtually, to ship back to Earth for sale to the highest bidder.

I glanced around my room. Small, uncluttered, with not an artifact of my own in it. I had passed every treasure across the desk to Zweig; I had no wish to retain any for myself. I sensed that the antiquarian urge was dying in me, choked to death by the wild commercialism that entangled me from the moment I signed the contract with the Company.

I picked up a book—Evans, *The Palace of Minos*—and looked at it balefully for a moment before replacing it on the shelf. My eyes throbbed from the day's anguish; I felt dried out and very tired.

Someone knocked at the door—timidly at first, then more boldly.

"Come in," I said.

The door opened slowly and a small Voltuscian stepped in. I recognized him—he was an unemployed guide, too unreliable to be trusted. "What do you want, Kushkak?" I asked wearily.

"Sir? Jarrell-sir?"

"Yes?"

"Do you need a boy, sir? I can show you the best treasures, sir. Only the best—the kind you get good price for."

"I have a guide already," I told him. "Dolbak. I don't need another, thanks."

The alien seemed to wrinkle in on himself. He hugged his lower arms to his sides unhappily. "Then I am sorry I disturbed you, Jarrell-sir. Sorry. Very sorry."

I watched him back out despairingly. All of these Voltuscians seemed to me like withered old men, even the young ones. They were an utterly decadent race, with barely a shred of the grandeur they must have had in the days when the great artifacts were being produced. It was odd, I thought, that a race should shrivel so in the course of a few thousand years.

The Artifact Business

I sank into an uneasy repose in my big chair. About half past twenty-three, another knock sounded.

"Come in," I said, a little startled.

The gaunt figure of George Darby stepped through the door. Darby was an archaeologist who shared many of my ideals, shared my passionate desire to see Earth, shared my distaste for the bondage into which we had sold ourselves.

"What brings *you* here so late, George?" I asked, adding the conventional "And how was your trip today?"

"My trip? Oh, my trip!" He seemed strangely excited. "Yes, my trip. You know my boy Kushkak?"

I nodded. "He was just here looking for a job. I didn't know he'd been working with you."

"Just for a couple of days," Darby said. "He agreed to work for five percent, so I took him on."

I made no comment. I knew how things could pinch.

"He was here, eh?" Darby frowned. "You didn't hire him, did you?"

"Of course not!" I said.

"Well, I did. But yesterday he led me in circles for five hours before admitting he didn't really have any sites in mind, so I canned him. And that's why I'm here."

"Why? Who'd you go out with today?"

"No one," Darby said bluntly. "I went out alone." For the first time, I noticed that his fingers were quivering, and in the dreary half-light of my room his face looked pale and drawn.

"You went out alone?" I repeated. "Without a guide?"

Darby nodded, running a finger nervously through his unruly white forelock. "It was half out of necessity—I couldn't find another boy in time—and half because I wanted to strike out on my own. The guides have a way of taking you to the same area of the Burial Ground all the time, you know. I headed in the other direction. Alone."

He fell silent for a moment. I wondered what it was that troubled him so.

After a pause he said, "Help me off with my knapsack."

I eased the straps from his shoulders and lowered the gray canvas bag to a chair. He undid the rusted clasps, reached in, and tenderly drew something out. "Here," he said. "What do you make of this, Jarrell?"

I took it from him with great care and examined it closely. It was a bowl, scooped by hand out of some muddy-looking black clay. Fingermarks stood out raggedly, and the bowl was unevenly shaped and awkward-looking. It was an extremely uncouth job.

"What is it?" I asked. "Prehistoric, no doubt."

Darby smiled unhappily. "You think so, Jarrell?"

"It must be," I said. "Look at it—I'd say it was made by a child, if it weren't for the size of these fingerprints in the clay. It's very ancient or else the work of an idiot."

He nodded. "A logical attitude. Only—I found this in the stratum *below* the bowl." And he handed me a gilded tooth-wedge in Third Period style.

"This was *below* the bowl?" I asked, confused. "The bowl is more recent than the tooth-wedge, you're saying?"

"Yes," he said quietly. He knotted his hands together. "Jarrell, here's my conjecture, and you can take it for as much as you think it's worth. Let's discount the possibility that the bowl was made by an idiot, and let's not consider the chance that it might be a representative of a decadent period in Voltuscian pottery that we know nothing about.

"What I propose," he said, measuring his words carefully, "is that the bowl dates from classical antiquity—three thousand years back, or so. And that the tooth-wedge you're admiring so is perhaps a year old, maybe two at the outside."

I nearly dropped the tooth-wedge at that. "Are you saying that the Voltuscians are hoaxing us?"

"I'm saying just that," Darby replied. "I'm saying that in those huts of theirs—those huts that are taboo for us to enter—they're busy turning out antiquities by the drove, and planting them in proper places where we can find them and dig them up."

It was an appalling concept. "What are you going to do?" I asked. "What proof do you have?"

"None, yet. But I'll get it. I'm going to unmask the whole filthy thing," Darby said vigorously. "I intend to hunt down Kushkak and throttle the truth out of him, and let the universe know that the Voltuscian artifacts are frauds, that the *real* Old Voltuscian artifacts are muddy, ugly things of no esthetic value and of no interest to—anyone—but—us—archaeologists," he finished bitterly.

"Bravo, George!" I applauded. "Unmask it, by all means. Let the greasy philistines who have overpaid for these pieces find out that they're *not* ancient, that they're as modern as the radiothermal stoves in their overfurnished kitchens. That'll sicken 'em—since they won't *touch* anything that's been in the ground less than a few millennia, ever since this revival got under way."

"Exactly," Darby said. I sensed the note of triumph in his voice. "I'll go out and find Kushkak now. He's just desperate enough to speak up. Care to come along?"

"No—no," I said quickly. I shun violence of any sort. "I've got some letters to write. You take care of it."

He packed his two artifacts up again, rose, and left. I watched him from my window as he headed across the unpaved streets to the liquor-dispensary where Kushkak was usually to be found. He entered—and a few minutes later I heard the sound of voices shouting in the night.

The news broke the next morning, and by noon the village was in a turmoil.

Kushkak, taken unawares, had exposed all. The Voltuscians—brilliant handicrafters, as everyone knew—had attempted to sell their work to the wealthy of Earth for years, but there had been no market. "Contemporary? Pah!" What the customers wanted was *antiquity*.

Unable to market work that was labelled as their own, the Voltuscians had obligingly shifted to the manufacture of antiquities, since their ancestors had been thoughtless enough not to leave them anything more marketable than crude clay pots. Creating a self-consistent ancient history that would appeal to the imaginations of Earthmen was difficult, but they rose to the challenge and developed one to rank with those of Egypt and Babylonia and the other fabled cultures of Earth. After that, it was a simple matter of designing and executing the artifacts.

Then they were buried in the appropriate strata. This was a difficult feat, but the Voltuscians managed it with ease, restoring the disrupted strata afterward with the same skill for detail as they employed in creating the artifacts. The pasture thus readied, they led the herd to feast.

I looked at the scrawny Voltuscians with new respect in

74

my eyes. Obviously they must have mastered the techniques of archaeology before inaugurating their hoax, else they would never have handled the strata relationships so well. They had carried the affair off flawlessly—until the day when one of the Earthmen had unkindly disinterred a *real* Voltuscian artifact.

Conditions were still chaotic when I entered the square in front of the assay office later that afternoon. Earthmen and Voltuscians milled aimlessly around, not knowing what to do next or where to go.

I picked up a rumor that Zweig was dead by his own hand, but this was promptly squelched by the appearance of the assayer in person, looking rather dreadfully upset but still living. He came to the front of the office and hung up a hastily-scrawled card. It read:

NO BUSINESS TRANSACTED TODAY

I saw Dolbak go wandering by and called to him. "I'm ready to go out," I said innocently.

He looked at me, pity in his lidless eyes. "Sir, haven't you *heard?* There will be no more trips to the Burial Grounds."

"Oh? This thing is true, then?"

"Yes," he said sadly. "It's true."

Obviously he couldn't bear to talk further. He moved on, and I spotted Darby.

"You seem to have been right," I told him. "The whole business has fallen apart."

"Of course. Once they were confronted with Kushkak's story, they saw the game was up. They're too fundamentally honest to try to maintain the pretense in the face of our accusation."

"It's too bad, in a way," I said. "Those things they turned out *were* lovely, you know."

"And the Piltdown Man had an interesting jawbone, too," Darby retorted hotly.

"Still," I said, "it's not as if the Voltuscians were being malicious about it. Our peculiarities of taste made it impossible for them to sell their goods honestly—so it was either do it dishonestly or starve. Weren't we caught in something of the same trap when we agreed to join the Company?"

"You're right there," Darby admitted reluctantly. "But—"

"Just a second, friend," said a deep voice from behind us. We turned to see David Sturges glaring at us bitterly.

"What do *you* want?" Darby asked.

"I want to know why you couldn't keep your mouth shut," said Sturges. "Why'd you have to ruin this nice setup for us? What difference did it make if the artifacts were the real thing or not? As long as the people on Earth were willing to lay down real cash for them, why rock the boat?"

Darby sputtered impotently at the bigger man, but said nothing.

"You've wrecked the whole works," Sturges went on. "What do you figure to do for a living now? Can you afford to go to some other planet?"

"I did what was right," Darby said.

Sturges snorted derisively and walked away. I looked at Darby. "He's got a point, you know. We're going to have to go to another planet now. Voltus isn't worth a damn.

The Artifact Business

You've succeeded in uprooting us and finishing the Voltuscian economy at the same time. Maybe you *should* have kept quiet."

He looked at me stonily for a moment. "Jarrell, I think I've overestimated you," he said.

A ship came for Zweig the next day, and the assay office closed down permanently. The Company wouldn't touch Voltus again. The crew of the ship went rapidly through the Terran outpost distributing leaflets that informed us that the Company still required our services and could use us on other planets—provided we paid our own fares.

That was the catch. None of us had saved enough, out of the fees we had received from the Company, to get off Voltus. It had been the dream of all of us to see Earth someday, to explore the world from which our parent stock sprang—but it had been a fool's dream. At Company rates, we could never save enough to leave.

I began to see that perhaps Darby *had* done wrong in exposing the hoax. It certainly didn't help us, and it was virtually the end of the world for the natives. In one swoop, a boundless source of income was cut off and their precarious economy totally wrecked. They moved silently through the quiet streets, and any day I expected to see the vultures perch on the rooftops. Honesty had been the worst policy, it seemed.

Three days after the bubble burst, a native boy brought me a note. It was from David Sturges, and it said, briefly, "There will be a meeting at my flat tonight at 1900. Sturges."

When I arrived, I saw that the entire little colony of

Company archaeologists was there—even Darby, who ordinarily would have nothing to do with Sturges.

"Good evening, Jarrell," Sturges said politely as I entered. "I think everyone's here now, and so we can begin." He cleared his throat.

"Gentlemen, some of you have accused me of being unethical," he said. "Even dishonest. You needn't deny it. I *have* been unethical. However," he said, frowning, "I find myself caught in the same disaster that has overtaken all of you, and just as unable to extricate myself. Therefore, I'd like to make a small suggestion. Accepting it will involve use of some of the—ah—moral flexibility you decry."

"What's on your mind, Sturges?" someone said impatiently.

"This morning," he said, "one of the aliens came to me with an idea. It's a good one. Briefly, he suggested that, as expert archaeologists, we teach the Voltuscians how to manufacture *Terran* artifacts. There's no more market for anything from Voltus—but why not continue to take advantage of the skills of the Voltuscians as long as the market's open for things of Earth? We could smuggle the artifacts to Earth, plant them, have them dug up again and sold there—and we'd make the entire profit, not just the miserable fee the Company allows us!"

"It's shady, Sturges," Darby said hoarsely. "I don't like the idea."

"How do you like the idea of starving?" Sturges retorted. "We'll rot on Voltus unless we use our wits."

I stood up. "Perhaps I can make things clearer to Dr. Darby," I said. "George, we're caught in a cleft stick and all we can do is try to wriggle. We can't get off Voltus, and we can't stay here. If we accept Sturges' plan, we'll build up a cash reserve in a short time. We'll be free to move on!"

Darby remained unconvinced. He shook his head. "I can't condone counterfeiting Terran artifacts. No—if you try it, I'll expose you!"

A stunned silence fell over the room at the threat. Sturges glanced appealingly at me, and I moistened my lips. "You don't seem to understand, George. Once we have this new plan working, it'll spur *genuine* archaeology. Look—we dig up half a dozen phony scarabs in the Nile Valley. People buy them—and we keep on digging, with the profits we make. Earth experiences a sudden interest; there's a rebirth of archaeology. We dig up *real* scarabs."

His eyes brightened, but I could see he was still unpersuaded. I added my clincher.

"Besides, George, someone will have to go to Earth to supervise this project." I looked around the room. "We'll have to pool our cash, won't we, to get a man down there?"

I paused, caught Sturges' silent approval. "I think," I said sonorously, "that it is the unanimous decision of this assembly that we nominate our greatest expert on Terran antiquity to handle the job on Earth—Dr. George Darby."

I didn't think he would be able to resist that. I was right. Suddenly, Darby stopped objecting.

Six months later, an archaeologist working near Gizeh turned up a scarab of lovely design, finely-worked and inlaid with strange jewels.

In a paper published in an obscure journal to which most of us subscribe, he conjectured that this find represented an outcrop of a hitherto-unknown area of Egyptology. He also sold the scarab to a jewelry syndicate for a staggering sum, and used the proceeds to finance an extensive exploration of the entire Nile Valley, something that hadn't been done since the decline of archaeology more than a century earlier.

Shortly afterward, a student working in Greece came up with a remarkable Homeric shield. Glazed pottery reached the light in Syria, and Scythian metalwork was exhumed in the wilds of the Caucasus. What had been a science as dead as alchemy suddenly blossomed into new life; the people of Earth discovered that their own world contained riches as desirable as those on Voltus and Dariak and the other planets the Company had been mining for gewgaws, and that they were somewhat less costly in the bargain.

The Voltuscian workshops are now going full blast, and the only limitation on our volume is the difficulty of smuggling the things to Earth and planting them. We're doing quite well financially, thank you. Darby, who's handling the job brilliantly on Earth, sends us a fat check every month, which we divide equally among ourselves after paying the happy Voltuscians.

Occasionally I feel regret that it was Darby and not myself who won the coveted job of going to Earth, but I reconcile myself with the awareness that there was no other way to gain Darby's sympathies. I've learned things about ends and means. Soon, we'll all be rich enough to travel to Earth, if we want to.

But I'm not so sure I *do* want to go. There was a *genuine* Voltuscian antiquity, you know, and I've become as interested in that as I am in that of Greece and Rome. I see an opportunity to do some pure archaeology in a virgin field of research.

So perhaps I'll stay here after all. I'm thinking of writing a book on Voltuscian artifacts—the *real* ones, I mean, all crude things of no commercial value whatever. And tomorrow I'm going to show Dolbak how to make Mexican pottery of the Chichimec period. It's attractive stuff. I think there ought to be a good market for it.

Precedent

On the second day of the third week since the Terran mission had arrived on Leeminorr, Lieutenant Blair Pickering committed an outrageous crime. Within an hour news of what Pickering had done had percolated back to the Terran base.

There, Colonel Lorne Norden studied the situation very carefully. Norden was commanding officer of the Terran Cultural and Military Mission on Leeminorr. The actions of his men were, ultimately, his responsibility. And since the Leeminorrans were touchy, formalistic, custom-bound people, highly conscious of the presence of Terrans among them, Norden gave the matter of Pickering's behavior particularly careful attention. He would have to make a decision in the case, and he knew clearly and well the consequences of a wrong-headed decision. The Corps kept careful records. There was a considerable body of precedent.

And precedent dictated special handling for the Pickering case.

Precedent

The incident had taken place shortly before noon—noon, the holiest hour on Leeminorr. Now, it was one-thirty; the midday repose was ended, and Norden knew it would not be long before indignant Leeminorrans arrived to begin filing their formal complaints.

The Terran camp was eight miles outside the town of Irkhiq, a village of perhaps three thousand Leeminorrans, built radially out from their temple. Norden's office was, coincidentally, located in the same relative position to the other Terran buildings as the Irkhiq temple was to the village surrounding it. It had been sheer accident—the master-plan for Cultural and Military outposts dictated the arrangement—but it had worked out well.

Norden himself waited patiently behind his desk for the first delegation to arrive. He was of medium height, but stocky and thick-muscled; for some reason his legs were short and dumpy, but when everyone was seated around a conference table Norden seemed the biggest man in the room. His hands were enormous; his forearms, massive and corded. He had been in the Service nineteen years. This was the eighth world on which he had served. He had taken his degree in Sociometrics at the University of Chicago in 2685, and five years later had won his commission in the Space Service Military Wing.

He made methodical, crisp notations in the log while waiting. Norden was not a man for brooding idly—and, as for developing a strategy to cope with the potentially explosive situation shaping up, he had done that a long time before.

At 1400 sharp his office communicator glowed. Norden reached smoothly for the stud, switched it on, and said: "Norden here. What goes?"

Precedent

"Five Leeminorrans here to see you, sir. They look disturbed. It's about this Pickering business, I think. Should I send them in?"

"At once."

Norden tidied his desk, swung around in his chair, and waited. After a moment the doorphone buzzed hestitantly, a timid droning sound.

"Come in," Norden said.

Five Leeminorrans entered, single file, their faces grave and severe. They arranged themselves in an open circle, their leader facing Norden, flanked by two of them at each side.

Norden had always felt faintly uncomfortable in the presence of the Leeminorrans. A short man himself, he had learned to feel distrust for taller people—and the Lee-minorrans were tall. They stood nearly seven feet in height, magnificent humanoid specimens with powerful-looking shoulders and brawny frames. Five of them, five males, in the discordantly-colored clothing of anger, savage reds shot through with raging violets and blacks. Their arms and legs were bare, allowing view of the superb muscles. The Leeminorrans had oiled themselves, applying the rancid animal fat that gave sheen and glow to their sleek metallic-blue skins.

Ten eyes, red-rimmed and feral, stared at him. Five lipless slitted mouths scowled down. Five angular-featured alien faces glowered at him. There was a long moment of silence in the room.

Five pairs of arms were extended in a ritual greeting: arms out, palms up, then fists clenched, biceps flexed. Impassively Norden watched the muscles bulge. Without rising, he acknowledged the greeting with three crisp, short Leeminorran syllables.

"You are Colonel Norden?" asked the foremost of the Leeminorrans. His voice was deep and big; it rattled in the cavern of his chest a moment before booming forth into the little room.

"I am," Norden said.

"I am Ahruntinok, Guardian of the Truth. I bring greetings from the Overman of Irkhiq, whose chosen representative I am."

Norden nodded. "The Overman is welcome here himself, of course."

"The Overman did not choose to come," replied Ahruntinok stonily. He gestured at his four companions. "I bring with me two priests of the temple, two servants of the Overman. They, too, offer you greetings."

The four flankers bent their knees solemnly, without speaking. Equally silently, Norden nodded response.

The preliminaries over, Ahruntinok glared down at Norden and said, "You have heard of what took place in Irkhiq this morning?"

"Perhaps. I heard what may have been a distorted account of the event. How does the Overman see it, Ahruntinok?"

"As blasphemy," came the flat, cold reply.

"Suppose you tell me what happened," Norden suggested. With a casual gesture of his left hand he flicked on the autotype; it would be important to have a recording of Ahruntinok's statement later, he knew.

The alien squinted suspiciously at the device as it came humming into life, but made no protest. He said, "It was morning in the village, the sun climbing high toward the top of the sky, when your Pickering and his men arrived in the small car you use for riding. They drove through the outer streets of Irkhiq as they do every morning. They passed the temple. It was nearly the moment of noon, when the sun's rays strike the front steps of the temple, purifying it for that day and making it possible for us to enter and pray.

"Several of us were there when Pickering came along. He entered the temple courtyard. He ignored the cries of the priests in attendance and passed over the steps *at the same moment as the rays of the sun!* Then he proceeded to sit on the steps, draw a food-pack from his uniform pocket, and eat. The priests continued to protest, but he paid no attention to them. When he was finished eating, he crumpled his refuse paper and left it where he sat; then he returned to his vehicle and rode away. The temple is polluted. The purification ceremony will take days."

Ahruntinok paused. His face was bleak; his arms were folded, one six-fingered hand grasping each elbow in an aggressive, accusing manner.

"Lieutenant Pickering has committed blasphemy," the alien said. "He must be tried in full court and punished for this, or else the temple's purification will be made much more difficult."

Norden closed his eyes for a moment—and when he opened them, they were hard and searching. "Pickering's in his quarters now. I haven't spoken to him yet. I want to hear his side of this case."

"How long will that take?"

"Are you in a hurry?"

"The people must travel to the next town to pray. We

86

wish to hold the trial tonight and carry out the sentence on him tomorrow. The Festival of Days is coming; Irkhiq would be forever disgraced if our temple were impure at festival time."

"I see. It'll be a quick trial, then. I suppose you have the verdict all prepared, and it's just a simple matter to run through the legal formalities."

"Lieutenant Pickering has committed blasphemy," the alien repeated sonorously. "The penalty for that is severe. And you Earthmen have agreed to abide by the laws of Leeminorr while you remain here. Surely you won't raise any objection to the trial?"

Norden smiled, but it was an unfriendly, business-like smile. "The implication's unwarranted, Ahruntinok. We've bound ourselves by precedent to abide by local law. If a member of this mission has broken the law, we have to let him be tried by Leeminorran courts. Naturally we're interested in getting a fair trial for our man."

"He will have justice," Ahruntinok said.

"Good. Come back in five hours and see me again. I'll have Pickering ready for you by then."

"Excellent."

The aliens went into the ritual farewell pattern. It took nearly five minutes before they were through flexing muscles, stooping, and praying. Then they turned and left Norden's office.

Norden sat perfectly still for perhaps thirty seconds, reviewing in his mind the conversation just concluded. He would have to report this to Earth, of course. Close contact with home base was an essential characteristic of this sort of work.

And home base would be interested. After four years,

another Markin case had finally come up. The Devall Precedent had taken effect: *if an Earthman breaks a law of the planet where he is stationed, the aliens have the right to request trial by their own legal processes.*

Colonel John Devall had put that rule on the books back in 2705, on the planet Markin, World 7 of System 1106-sub-a. Devall had created a precedent, and it was intrinsic to the nature of the Terran missions to alien worlds that precedents be obeyed. Earth had to appear to the lesser worlds who received Earth's aid as an unchangeable, perfectly consistent culture—otherwise, there might be large-scale distrust.

If an Earth mission on one planet behaved in a certain manner, the other Earth missions would have to conform. It was necessary to present unity of objective as a characteristic of Earthmen.

Devall had set a precedent. *And,* thought Norden, *we're stuck with it!*

Strictly speaking, the parallel did not hold true in all respects. The earlier case had been somewhat different.

According to the tapes of the Devall case, a member of the Terran mission to Markin—a Lieutenant Paul Leonards, botanist—had been on a field trip with two other Earthmen. Discovering a secluded grove, they entered it and proceeded to photograph and take samples from any previously unknown botanical specimens. Suddenly they had been challenged by an armed alien; he attacked violently, ignoring a command by Lieutenant Leonards to lower his spear and explain his actions. When he charged with the spear, the Lieutenant had been forced to kill him in self-defense.

Precedent

But then complications began when the Earthmen returned to their base. Protesting aliens declared Leonards had entered a sacred grove and had slain the guardian. They demanded the right to try the Earthman by an ecclesiastical court.

It was then that Colonel Devall had made his famous decision. Devall had been an anthropologist, with a competent though undistinguished service record that had seen him lead missions to eleven worlds.

The problem had never come up before in the great Terran aid program. The aliens refused to listen to the argument that Leonards had had no way of knowing he was trespassing on sacred ground, and that he had killed the guardian only in self-defense. Intent had no place in Markin law; only the sheer pragmatic fact of the law-violation itself concerned them, and that had to be requited.

In the end Devall had handed Leonards over for trial, as the aliens requested. Devall had considered the matter long and deeply, and had concluded that in the spirit of fairness this was the only thing he could do. The Terrans lived among the aliens, and, reasoned Devall, they should therefore be bound by their laws.

Luckily, the Lieutenant had escaped serious harm. It had been trial by ordeal, and they had thrown him in a lake and left him to the mercies of two of the dead man's brothers. But he had outswimmed them, reached safety, and thus was declared not guilty.

Norden was familiar with the case. It was classic in the Corps' annals. He had pondered its implications, second-guessed Colonel Devall, thought the thing through with dogged detailed analysis.

Precedent

And now his turn had come. Lieutenant Pickering of his staff had blasphemed—not accidentally, as had the man on Markin, but knowingly.

The aliens were aware of the Markin precedent. They were anxious to try an Earthman.

Well, thought Norden, *they'll get their wish. Pickering is theirs to try. Let them hold us to the Devall Precedent—but they may not like it!*

Norden made some log notations, finishing off his weather report and adding three or four references to general mission progress, on the several fronts of survey work, anthropological research, and technological-medical aid. Each mission had a threefold job, and was staffed to handle it. It carried out an exhaustive botanical and zoological survey of the planet, taking as many specimens as possible; it performed cultural research among the inhabitants; and—on those worlds where the natives would permit it—Terran experts offered assistance in raising living standards.

At the same time, of course, an assessment of the planet's military value was made. It was a precautionary move. The galaxy was a near-infinite place; there was no telling when or from where a hostile and dangerous race might arrive, and it helped to have a network of friendly allies spread out across thousands of light-years.

Earth had never run across a world that was its equal technologically or philosophically; whether it was a matter of earlier evolution or luck along the way was impossible to determine, but the fact was undeniable that of the several thousand inhabited worlds visited by the survey teams in the four centuries since the development of interstellar travel, not one had reached a cultural level on a plane with Earth's.

An aid program, then, was a logical necessity. But it had to be handled with tact; sheer altruism was a difficult concept to put across, at times.

Norden finished his morning's work and restored the log to its file. Then, closing down the office equipment, he headed out into the chill Leeminorran afternoon. A bitter wind was blowing, tossing swept-up gusts of snow about in the compound. Harsh dark clouds drifted overhead, and far off near the mountaintops, inches above the horizon, Norden saw the bleak unwarm brightness of Leeminorr's unfriendly sun.

This was a hard, infertile world. The Leeminorrans were sturdy people who gloried in exposing their bodies to the elements, whose philosophy was based on conflict, and whose lives were battle-studded and tough. This was not a mechanically advanced world; communication was poor, transportation crude though adequate. The Leeminorrans recognized the need for the aid the Terrans offered, but they fought hard to maintain their ability and aloofness even while receiving help. An important part of Norden's job was to see to it that the Terran assistance program never began to seem to the Leeminorrans like a distribution of largesse.

He turned off at the communications center. Norden nodded to the signal officer and said, "Has that subradio solidophone contact with Earth come through yet?"

"Just about to call you, sir. Director Thornton's waiting to see you."

Precedent

"Thanks," Norden replied curtly, and stepped into the green lambency of the solido field.

Director Thornton sat back of a dark-grained bare desk ornamented in the Kauolanii tradition. He was a lean man, well along in years, thin-lipped, tight-faced, with a dry weather-hewn look about him.

He and Norden knew each other well. Norden had served under him on his own break-in cruise, long before Thornton had gone to Rio de Janeiro to take over the all-important post as Director of the Department of Extraterrestrial Affairs. Now Thornton sat poised, unspeaking, unsmiling, waiting to hear what Norden had to say to him.

The Colonel said, "It happened, finally. Another Devall affair."

Thornton smiled emotionlessly. "I had been wondering how long it would take. It's so easy to trespass on territory whose laws we hardly understand. The surprising thing is that this is only the second time."

"The aliens were here to see me not long ago. Naturally they demand the same privilege Devall granted on Markin. It's another blasphemy case."

"Of course," Thornton said. "The Leeminorrans are at the same general cultural-level as the Marks. At that stage they're likely to be highly blasphemy-conscious. When's the trial?"

"Tomorrow, probably. They'll be back to get the man soon. A full report's on its way to you via autotype. It ought to reach you soon."

Thornton nodded. "What action have you taken, Colonel?"

"The man will be handed over for trial—naturally. I

don't feel called on to deviate from the Devall Precedent. The aliens expect that kind of treatment."

"Naturally."

"There may be some outcry on Earth, sir. I'd like to request that you refrain from announcing anything about the trial until its conclusion."

Director Thornton looked doubtful. "It's not our usual policy to suppress news, Colonel. Is there some special reason for this request?"

"There is," Norden replied. "I'd prefer to wait until I have more definite data on the problem here." He stared levelly at Thornton and added, "In the sake of preventing future Devall Precedents. My actions will bind all my successors. I'd like to simplify things for them—and help the Leeminorrans at the same time."

Thornton ran his thin fingers along the elegantly-carved rim of his desk a moment or two, considering Norden's request. A smile spread slowly over his features.

"Very well, Colonel. Request granted. I'll maintain a news-curtain over the Leeminorran situation until hearing from you again. Report to me when the trial's over, of course."

"Yes, sir. Thank you, sir."

Norden stepped back out of the fading field. The last he saw of Director Thornton before the solidophone pattern shattered was the director's face, smiling encouragingly. It was not often that Thornton smiled.

Norden pulled his jumper tight around him and stepped out into the chilly wind.

Thornton had understood him—the smile said as much. Now it was Norden's turn to smile.

Precedent

An organization such as the Corps operated on precedent. Precedents, then, were not to be broken lightly.

But, thought Norden, there was nothing in the rules against *bending* them a little.

The delegation from Irkhiq was back at sundown, only this time there were six of them. Ahruntinok led the way, striding magnificently into the compound wearing a blazing red cloak twined with vruuk-feathers and tinged with gold; behind him came the two representatives of the priesthood, the two delegates from the secular government, and a sixth figure, gaunt and bowed.

Watching from the window of his office as the group entered the compound, Norden turned his attention particularly to this sixth man. He was old, much older than any of the other five, and yet he still had majesty in his stride even though his shoulders now sloped in and downward, even though his skin had lost the radiant gleam of young warriorhood.

He wore rich robes, draped thickly over his angular body—but his arms and legs were bare, in Leeminorran fashion, and on them Norden could see the welts and scars of a lifetime of combat. He walked slowly, with a steady tread, and held himself proudly erect. *This one was a man, once,* Norden thought. *He knew how to fight.*

The men were gathering around the compound, watching the slow procession with interest. Norden saw Gomez, the anthropologist in charge, surreptitiously snap a tridim shot of the sextet as they stalked past. The sun was down, and night was coming billowing in; the compound lights were on. Above, the tiny splinter of gleaming rock that was

94

Precedent

Leeminorr's sole excuse for a moon was rising across the sky, beginning its retrograde evening's course.

The thermometer just outside the window read 32°. Not cold, really, but certainly uninviting enough weather—but there was that old alien, looking seventy or eighty or perhaps ninety, strutting up the hill with arms and legs exposed. These were tough customers, Norden admitted admiringly.

The Leeminorrans reached the top of the little rise and gathered there, waiting. Ahruntinok stood facing Norden's two-story residence, staring in; Norden wondered whether the alien could see him, even in the darkness of twilight. He waited; after a moment he saw Reilly, the chief linguist, hesitantly approach the aliens.

They spoke with each other a few moments, with much bowing and gesticulating. Then Reilly detached himself from the group and crossed the clearing to Norden's place.

Norden met him at the door.

"What did they say?"

"They're here to get Pickering," Reilly explained. "But first they want you to come out and greet them. I told them I'd let you know."

"I'm on my way," Norden said. He slipped into his outer jacket and followed the linguist outside. Night was falling rapidly; he felt the cold whipping through him, whistling against his legs. He felt uncomfortable about greeting the aliens standing up: sitting down, he could more than hold his own, but the difference in height of more than a foot discomforted him when they met outdoors.

He reached the group and Ahruntinok offered a ritual greeting. Norden responded.

"The trial will be held tomorrow," Ahruntinok said. "I

have brought the judge." He indicated the old man. "Mahr-lek, Grand Judge of Irkhiq. He will pass judgment on the Earthman."

The battle-scarred oldster lowered himself in an elaborate bow; Norden did his best to return it, while the five other aliens glowered sourly at him.

"You will give us the man Pickering now," said Ahruntinok when the greeting was concluded. "Tonight he must remain in Irkhiq. Tomorrow will be the trial."

"Where will the trial be held?" Norden asked.

"Irkhiq. Before the temple. The entire village will be present."

Norden was silent for a moment. At length he said, "Of course, other Earthmen can attend the trial?"

Ahruntinok's face darkened. He said, "There is nothing prohibiting their presence. You will not be permitted to interfere with the trial."

"I simply want to watch it," Norden said.

The big alien snorted suspiciously. The old judge stepped to the fore and said, "The night grows cold. Give us the prisoner."

Norden wondered how Devall had faced the actual moment of transfer of possession, when the life of a Terran was given over into alien hands. It must have been a bleak moment for the man.

He turned and caught sight of Sergeant Heong standing some forty feet away, taking down the proceedings with a portable recorder.

"Heong, go get Lieutenant Pickering," Norden ordered crisply.

"Yes, sir."

Leaving the recorder on, Heong set out across the yard

on a jog trot toward the officers' barracks, where Pickering had been confined pending resolution of the case. Norden saw the Sergeant pounding at the door; then he disappeared within, returning a moment later followed by the bulky figure of Lieutenant Blair Pickering.

The wind swept low over the camp as Pickering appeared. Norden shivered involuntarily; the temperature was beginning its nightly drop. By 2200 or so, the thermometer would be hovering close to zero, and the wind would shriek like a tormented demon all the bleak night.

Heong and Pickering drew near. The lieutenant was in full uniform, braid and all, though he had left off the ornamental blaster. His boots were polished to mirror intensity; he looked fresh and imposing.

For a moment Norden and Pickering eyed each other. Pickering was a big man, with all of Norden's swelling muscularity plus the long legs that should have been his; he stood six-four, big enough by Norden's standards but still nearly half a foot shorter than Ahruntinok. His face was dark and shadowy, craggy-featured, with a thick beak of a nose mounted slightly askew. He had no scientific specialty; he was one of the base's military attachés, one of a complement of six.

The cold air seemed to transmit an electric crackle of tension. Pickering stood stiffly at attention, staring up at the group of aliens. Norden tried to picture him swaggering into town, cavalierly crossing the threshold of the temple at the very moment the seldom-seen purifying rays of the sun were about to strike it, then contemptuously unpacking and eating his lunch in this most sacred of Leeminorran sanctuaries.

It had been an outrage. And Pickering looked hardly

contrite as he stood in the whistling wind, jaw set tightly, arms stiff at his sides.

"At ease, Lieutenant," Norden said.

Pickering sullenly let his shoulders slump, his feet slip apart.

"Pickering, I'm placing you in the custody of this group of Leeminorrans. The man in charge is Ahruntinok, who was appointed Guardian of the Truth by the Overman of Irkhiq. Roughly speaking, he's the prosecuting attorney. This gentleman here is Mahrlek, the Grand Judge who'll try your case."

"Yes, sir," Pickering said tonelessly,

"The trial will be held tomorrow. I'll be present at it, Lieutenant. I've reported details of this case to Director Thornton on Earth."

Norden glanced at the aliens. "He's in your hands. What time does the trial begin?"

"Be there at sunup," Ahruntinok said, "if you wish to be present."

Sunup—and, for the second time in history, a human's life lay in the hands of an alien court of law.

Norden had risen at sunup every day of his adult life; this was no exception. The thermometer showed 24°; dawn was breaking over the wall of mountains to the distant east.

He dressed rapidly. The men who were accompanying him had been picked the night before, their names posted on the camp bulletin board; they were dressed and ready early. Norden saw them gathered round a jeep in the middle of the compound, waiting for him.

A quick splash of depilator took care of his stubbly face.

Precedent

He adjusted his uniform, glanced at his watch, and signalled through the window that he was on his way out.

They made the trip virtually in silence, down the winding rutted road that led from the Terran camp to the village of Irkhiq. There were six in the car; Sergeant Heong drove, and along with Norden came anthropologist Gomez, linguist Reilly, Lieutenant Thomas of the Military Wing staff, and Technical Assistant Lennon.

The eight-mile trip ended, finally; the jeep turned off into the broad road that led through town to the temple. The streets were deserted all the way—and for good reason, Norden saw, as they came within sight of the centrally-located temple; the entire village had come out as advertised to see the trial. Three thousand of them, packed tightly together in the square that faced Irkhiq's temple.

The temple was a blocky unpretty building perhaps a hundred feet high, surmounted by an off-center spire. Architecture on Leeminorr had never amounted to much. The temple opened out on a wide courtyard, and three great stone steps gave access to the inner areas. It was on those steps that Pickering had allegedly blasphemed and committed sacrilege, and it was on those steps that he was being tried.

No one occupied the courtyard behind the steps. The temple was polluted, and until the purification ceremonies were complete no public services could be held there.

Pickering stood between two towering Leeminorran guards. He was still in his uniform—it looked as if he'd slept in it, or if he hadn't been to sleep at all. He needed a shave. His dark craggy face was scowling, but he remained stiffly at attention; his guards were armed with drawn wide-bladed krisses, and they looked willing to use them at any provocation. Both of them topped seven feet. Pickering was oddly dwarfed between them.

Fanning out to the accused man's right and left were two files of bright-clad priests; back of them stood civil police and local functionaries. Three Leeminorrans sat in a little triangle facing Pickering, in an open space some twenty feet square. At the foremost vertex of the triangle sat Mahrlek, the Grand Judge; behind him and to the left was Ahruntinok, Guardian of the Truth, and next to him, resplendent in his robes of state, was the immense figure of Him, the nameless priest-king, the village Overman— He who gave up his name when he assumed his exalted rank, lest demons learn the true name of the Overman and work harm to the village.

The Earthmen rode their jeep as far as possible toward the temple; when the assembled crowd grew too thick to allow further progress, Norden said, "We'd better get out and walk," and they did.

The throng seemed to melt away on both sides of them as they marched single-file inward toward the temple steps. Passing between the rows of huge aliens was like walking through a field of corn in late summer; even the women were six-footers and better.

They reached the trial area. The trio in the clearing sat quite motionless; Pickering might have been a statue on the temple steps.

Suddenly the Overman rose and spread his arms wide, upward, encompassing the entire group, it seemed. When he spoke, his voice was a pealing basso that rolled out over their heads and seemed to crash against the mountain wall that ringed in the entire Irkhiq district.

Precedent

"Children of light
Children of darkness
Attend here this day
To see justice done.
That which is wrong
Will be made right
That which is soiled
Will be made clean.
Begin."

When the final harsh syllable of the invocation had died away, Ahruntinok rose. The Guardian of the Truth was nearly the size of the Overman, but he lacked the awesome presence of the other. He said, simply, "The man from beyond the skies has blasphemed. We gather here today to pass sentence on him, to offer him to justice, to cleanse the temple. The white light of justice will prevail."

At Norden's side, Lieutenant Thomas whispered, "I thought this was supposed to be a *trial,* sir. The way these guys are acting, Pickering's guilt's a matter of common knowledge, and they're here to pass sentence!"

Norden nodded. "I'm aware of that, Lieutenant. Leeminorran law isn't necessarily the same as Earth's. But don't worry."

The two files of priests burst into an antiphony now, the right-hand side giving forth a melismatic line of verse, the left-hand side picking it up on the fourth accented syllable and repeating it. It was not quite singing, not quite speech—an elaborate *sprechstimme* that continued for nearly five minutes in close harmony. Pickering stood frozen as the waves of sound washed over him from right and left, as if bathing him.

101

Precedent

The prayer ended. Ahruntinok rose again and recited an account of Pickering's crime, phrasing it in a highly inflected antique manner that was probably the legal dialect on Leeminorr. Norden followed it, but with difficulty; if he had not already been familiar with the facts in the case, he might have been hard put to understand what the Guardian of the Truth was saying.

When Ahruntinok was finished the choir of priests responded with another chanted prayer—a monody this time, slow and grave, building to a moody introverted series of minor-key ejaculations. Norden was glad he had ordered Heong to carry a pocket recorder; in all probability this would be their only chance to record this form of Leeminorran musical art.

Norden glanced at his watch. It was 0800—the trial had been proceeding for more than an hour now—and still not a word had been said in Pickering's defense. The Leeminorran concept of legal form was surprising, but not overly so. This was a rugged people; an offender caught in the act was due for a rugged trial.

For a third time Ahruntinok rose. This time the Guardian of the Truth reviewed the nature of Pickering's offense in five or six terse sentences—*for the benefit of the villagers,* Norden thought, *or perhaps for the benefit of us*—and then stepped forward until he was no more than half a dozen feet from the motionless Pickering.

"The temple must be purified. The crime of blasphemy must be washed away. The demon must be driven from this man who stands on the temple steps.

"Prayers and incense will purify the temple. Prayers and incense will cleanse the village of blasphemy. But only the whip will drive out a demon!"

Precedent

The priests echoed Ahruntinok's last three sentences. It sounded to Norden like nothing so much as a big scene from *Aida*—one where Radames stands accused. Obviously the "trial" had been carefully rehearsed.

The villagers took it up next. *"Prayers and incense will purify the temple! Prayers and incense will cleanse the village of blasphemy! But only the whip will drive out a demon!"*

Norden glanced at Pickering. The condemned man was utterly emotionless; his jaw was set, his lips clamped, as he listened to the exulting outcry.

Ahruntinok said, "I call now upon the Grand Judge of the village of Irkhiq."

Mahrlek rose.

The old man stepped forward into the place vacated by Ahruntinok. He waited—one minute, two, until the tension drew so tight the ground seemed ready to split under the strain. Finally he lifted his hands overhead, holding them rock-steady, and brought them swiftly down.

A shout went up from the populace.

Mahrlek said, "The temple must be purified. The blasphemy must be driven from the air of the village. He who is possessed by a demon must be cured. Let the demon be exorcized. Let the Earthman be driven once around the village boundaries by men with whips."

Norden felt Lieutenant Thomas nudge him sharply. "Sir, that's murder! They'll whip him to death!"

"Quiet," Norden whispered.

Pickering was staring stonily forward. There was even the beginning of a smile on his face.

Norden held his breath. He had coached Pickering well for this moment; if only they had the ritual down straight—!

103

Precedent

In a quiet but authoritative voice Pickering said, "I swear by the sun and the sky, by the mountains and by the snow, that there is no demon in me."

His statement was followed by a sudden moment of shocked silence—broken by a gasp of astonishment that became thunderous when multiplied by three thousand throats.

Ahruntinok was on his feet again, his face purpling; all the Guardian of the Truth's calm of a moment before had vanished. "Impossible! Impossible! How can he make such an oath? How can a demon-possessed one swear by the holy and blessed?"

The chorus of priests had disintegrated into a knot of argumentative theologians. A hot buzz of comment drifted from them. Norden smiled in relief; it had gone across, then. The paradox had been hurled forth.

They were all on their feet now—the Overman, the Grand Judge, Ahruntinok—staring at Pickering. The guards at Pickering's sides tightened their grips on their blades, but superstitiously moved several feet away.

The Grand Judge advanced on wobbly legs. He detached the jewel-encrusted cowl he wore round his neck and extended it nape-first to Pickering.

"Touch your hands to this and repeat what you just said," Mahrlek ordered in a quavering voice.

Pickering smiled bleakly, grasped the Cowl of Justice, and repeated his statement. The old judge ripped the cowl away and hastily tottered back.

Utter confusion prevailed in the trial area. Norden had chosen his steps wisely. He picked this moment to come forward, jostling his way through the horde of open-mouthed villagers, and entered the cleared area.

Precedent

"As leader of the Earthmen I claim the right to speak on this matter here and now!"

He glanced in appeal at the Overman.

"Speak," the Overman said hoarsely.

"You have given my man trial by your own ways, and you find he is possessed by a demon. But the oath he has just sworn is one no demon could swear. Is this right?"

The trio of Leeminorrans nodded reluctantly.

"The court is thus in doubt. According to your own law, there is only one way this case may be settled now. I call for that method!"

The aliens exchanged glances. "The trial by combat?" Mahrlek asked querulously.

"Yes," Norden said. "The trial by combat, with Pickering fighting the Guardian of the Truth to determine where justice truly lies in this matter!"

The Overman laughed—a welling crescendo of ironic amusement. His face dissolved into a hundred wrinkling laugh-lines; his body shook.

"Your man—against Ahruntinok?"

"Yes," Norden said.

The Overman gestured, and Ahruntinok crossed the clearing to stand facing Pickering. The Guardian of the Truth was six inches taller than the Earthman, and at least a hundred pounds heavier.

"This is amusing," the Overman said. "But justice must be served. Your choice of weapons?"

"Bare hands," Norden said. "Body against body. Fist against fist."

He looked at Pickering, who merely nodded slightly without otherwise indicating reaction.

105

Precedent

"Body against body," the Overman repeated. "Fist against fist."

The Grand Judge said, "It will be the simplest way. The Earthman is mad; this will demonstrate it. And the law calls for such a thing."

For a moment the Overman seemed deep in thought; he stood facing Norden like a slumbering volcano, brooding, eyes turned inward. After a long pause he said, "So be it. Ahruntinok will combat with the Earthman Pickering— naked, on the gaming-ground of Mount Zcharlaad. Justice will be served. The defeat of the Earthman will serve to purify and cleanse us. And then we can drive forth the demon who confuses our trial and bedevils us all."

He pointed toward the Guardian of the Truth. "Ahruntinok, is this trial agreeable to you?"

Ahruntinok grinned. "I welcome it."

"And to you, Earthman?"

Pickering shrugged. "I'll fight him," he said, without altering his sullen expression.

"It is decreed, then." The Overman turned to face the throng. "We shall adjourn to the gaming-ground of Mount Zcharlaad!"

It took nearly half an hour for the crowd to disperse. Norden, Pickering, the three high Leeminorrans, and the five other Earthmen remained in a loose grouping around the temple steps, waiting for the mob to break up.

Little was said. The aliens exchanged a few puzzled whispers, but Norden was unable to hear what they were saying. He could bet on it, though: they were wondering how Pickering had been able to confound their theology so

106

thoroughly. Obviously he was demon-possessed, or else he would never have committed his acts of sacrilege—but yet, no demon could have sworn innocence on the cowl of the Grand Judge. It made no sense. Trial by combat was the simplest solution. If Ahruntinok trounced the Earthman, as seemed most likely, then Pickering was guilty of malicious and deliberate acts against the Leeminorran religion, and the beating he would get from Ahruntinok would be ample punishment. But if Pickering should win—

Norden guessed that the Leeminorrans preferred not to speculate about *that* possibility.

He waited, saying nothing. Pickering stood between his two guards, unsmiling. Finally the time to depart came.

Norden left Pickering behind in custody of the aliens, since he was still nominally a prisoner of theirs. He led the way back to the jeep and they piled in, Heong behind the wheel.

As the turbos thrummed into life, Lieutenant Thomas, the Military Wing attaché, swiveled round to look at Norden, who sat in the back.

"Sir?"

"What is it, Lieutenant?"

"Would you mind explaining the facets of this trial to me? I'm afraid I got lost six or seven turns back, when the prosecuting attorney was still yowling for Pickering's scalp. How come you stepped in and demanded this trial by combat thing?"

The Lieutenant was red-faced; he was acutely conscious, evidently, that he was the only man in the jeep without formal scientific training, and it was rough on him to sit there with his ignorance showing.

Precedent

Norden said, "Would you have preferred it if I'd kept quiet and let them whip Pickering to death?"

"No, sir—but—sir, it's just as bad this way! That alien must be six foot ten, six-eleven, and close to four hundred pounds. It'll be slaughter, sir!"

"You think so? Watch, then," Norden said, grinning. "Pickering's no midget at six-four."

"He is next to that boy, sir!"

"You watch, Lieutenant. I think I know what I'm doing."

There wasn't much that could be said after that. Norden sat quietly, staring through the jeep window at the steadily more forbidding landscape; they were rising through some rocky country now, following the broad back of a large Leeminorran vehicle bulging with townspeople. The Leeminorrans still used internal-combustion engines for their cars; it made an unholy racket.

They wound upward along the mountain path. The ground was covered with a thick layer of snow, and a vicious wind whined down from the sawtooth crests of the upjutting, unforested mountains. It was hard to believe that this was Leeminorran summer; in the winter, in this continent, temperatures rarely rose above freezing, and in the mountains the thermometer stayed between zero and eighty or ninety below for nine months of the year . . . getting as "warm" as freezing for a brief hot spell in midsummer.

Norden reviewed the steps of the trial in his mind. His report would need to be done with care; it was going to be a document given to every Corps trainee to read, along with Colonel Devall's report that preceded it. The reports would make an interesting pair side by side, he thought.

The Norden Precedent. He liked the sound of that.

Precedent

He smiled. There would be plenty of theological discussing going on tonight in the village of Irkhiq, he thought. Plenty.

In fact, it was going to take more than one evening to get everything straightened around, theologically. The Leeminorrans might even need a brand new theology before Norden got through with them.

The gaming-ground of Mount Zcharlaad was a broad plateau-like area set in an outstretched arm of the sprawling mountain, at an elevation of perhaps five thousand feet. Norden was grateful for that; much higher up, it might have been too rough on Pickering.

A natural amphitheater ringed the site, a shell-like rise in the rock into which seats had been hewn. Now the villagers filed slowly into the seats. A layer of snow covered the gaming-ground itself, and a bitter wind sliced downward from the higher reaches of the mountain chain.

Pickering did not look worried. He stamped his feet a few times against the cold, but otherwise seemed calm, almost *too* calm. It might have been a fatalistic numbness, Norden thought.

Ahruntinok looked elated. The big alien had already stripped down to his fighting costume—a pair of woven briefs and sandal-like buskins—and was loosening up, flexing his huge muscles, swaggering around the outside of the ring, clenching and unclenching his fists. The cold hardly bothered him. His dull-blue skin was glowing healthily, and his features were animated. Norden wondered how many times Ahruntinok had fought here in the gaming-grounds; not a few, he supposed.

Precedent

The Grand Judge and the Overman stood silently to Norden's side. Their faces revealed little of any thought patterns behind them.

"When does it start?" Norden asked finally.

"Soon," the Grand Judge said. He pointed to the tiny dot that was the sun, hovering just above the crests of the mountains, and said, "The time is not yet right. A few moments more. A few moments more."

Norden walked over to Pickering. "All set, Lieutenant? Feeling all right?"

"Fine, sir."

"The cold won't bother you, now?"

"It may slow me up a little. I'm not worried about it, sir. I can manage."

"I hope so," Norden said. He glanced up at the big man —who seemed so strangely dwarfed by the towering Leeminorrans—and grinned. "Good luck, Pickering."

"Thanks, sir."

The Grand Judge signalled. It was time for the bout to begin.

He stepped forward. In a surprisingly ringing voice, old Mahrlek announced, "Justice now will be served. Ahruntinok, Guardian of the Truth, will meet in combat the Earthman Pickering."

Priests stationed in the first row of seats set up a wailing ululation of a chant. *Ahruntinok's cheerleaders, no doubt,* Norden thought.

Pickering stripped down to fighting costume—shorts and boots, nothing else. No tape on the fists, no gloves, no masks. Just two naked men against each other, in forty-degree weather, with no holds barred. *Justice will be served here today.*

Precedent

The priestly chanting reached a wild climax, tenors and basses shrieking in utter atonal discordancy on the final three notes.

Then the gaming-grounds became very silent.

"Justice will be served," said the Grand Judge in solemn, sententious tones.

The fighters stepped forward.

Ahruntinok gleamed with oil; his hairless body shone in the faint sunlight, and his muscles stood out against his sleek skin in sharp relief. He was grinning, showing his mouthful of spadeshaped teeth; he stepped toward the center of the gaming area with a wide rolling walk, like a sailor heading downship in a fierce storm.

Pickering was in the center already, and waiting, poised. His unanointed body had little of Ahruntinok's glamor; he looked too pale, too hairy, too squat and clumsy next to the Guardian of the Truth. Ahruntinok moved with the grace of a well-oiled killing machine; Pickering, with the awkward ponderous notions of an ancient tank. The only sound was the whistling of the wind.

Ahruntinok broke the silence with three quick grunted guttural syllables: a challenge, perhaps, or an invocation, a prayer. Pickering remained silent.

Arms wide, Ahruntinok moved forward.

Norden saw the strategy at once. Ahruntinok intended to make the most efficient use of his half-foot advantage in size and reach, and of his great weight. He was going to hug Pickering to him, draw the Earthman into a bearlike grip and squeeze him into unconsciousness or death.

Ahruntinok's red-rimmed eyes flashed savagely. He advanced toward Pickering, reaching out to gather the Earthman in.

111

Precedent

But Pickering had other ideas. He danced forward into the spreading hoop of Ahruntinok's arms and smashed a fist upward at the square chin of the Guardian of the Truth; then he spun away, quickly, slipping beneath the big alien's guard.

Ahruntinok bellowed in anger and whirled on Pickering. A second time the Earthman tiptoed forward and landed a punch, skipping away untouched. Murmurs began to pass through the watching crowd.

The alien had shown no ill effects as a result of Pickering's two punches, but he was angry. He thundered toward the Earthman now, arms flailing, huge fists whistling through the air. Pickering easily avoided one wild swing that would have been fatal had it landed, and cracked his left fist into Ahruntinok's exposed belly. A gust of air escaped from the alien's mouth.

Ahruntinok howled. The warrior's nobility was gone; he reached out desperately with clawed fingertips and managed to scratch six red lines down Pickering's shoulder— but at the same time the Earthman casually slapped an open-handed blow at Ahruntinok's mouth, and a dribble of red blood trickled forth, running down the alien's chin.

Now the crowd was silent again—*frightened* silent.

Pickering exhaled a cloud of white fog and called out to the alien. Ahruntinok whirled; Pickering hit him with a sharp left to the heart, followed with a savagely aimed right smash that sent Ahruntinok's head snapping back.

Norden, at the sidelines, felt a sudden burst of exultation. *The bigger they are,* he thought—

Ahruntinok was utterly disorganized. He had never been able to get his superb body unhooked and ready for action;

112

Precedent

Pickering now seemed all about him, lashing him with blows from every direction at once. Ahruntinok was growling angrily, sending panicky swipes in hopes of felling Pickering with a sudden blow, but he was unable to land any.

Pickering was everywhere. The six-inch height differential mattered very little now. One of Ahruntinok's eyes was swelling shut, now; the other was bruised. The alien's thin lips were split. Sweat washed down his massive shoulders and back, mixed with blood.

Ahruntinok was a wrestler, and a fine one. But the first rule of wrestling is that you have to get hold of your man before you can do any damage to him. And Pickering moved too quickly for that.

Ahruntinok was turning in circles, howling like a blinded Polyphemus, imploring Pickering to come within range of his crushing grip. Pickering did—just long enough to detonate an uprising right off the point of Ahruntinok's chin. The giant wobbled; Pickering lifted another from the floor and Ahruntinok staggered forward, still conscious, blood and spittle foaming from his mouth.

Norden glanced at the Overman. He looked sick.

Ahruntinok dropped wearily to his knees and straggled toward Pickering, groping for him. Pickering ran forward and slapped Ahruntinok twice, fast, to keep him conscious a while longer. The alien rocked and tried to take his feet again; Pickering grabbed one of Ahruntinok's arms and whipped it up suddenly behind the giant's back.

Norden wondered if they'd invented the half-nelson on Leeminorr. If they hadn't, they were in for an enlightening sight now.

With his free arm Ahruntinok vainly tried to catch hold

of Pickering, who stood just behind him. Pickering proved uncatchable. He bent Ahruntinok's arm higher, higher, holding it now in an unbreakable grip.

Norden had never heard three thousand more silent people in his life.

Pickering was grinning savagely now. Norden saw that he had absorbed a few bruises in the contest himself; one lip was puffy, and his left ear was swollen. But generally he seemed in good shape. He yanked Ahruntinok's arm up. The giant grunted.

A single loud *crack!* resounded over the gaming-grounds.

Pickering released Ahruntinok's suddenly limp arm and stood back as the giant writhed in pain, knotting his huge legs as if wishing he had Pickering's neck imprisoned between his tightening thighs. Pickering grasped Ahruntinok's other arm and glanced questioningly at Norden.

Norden shook his head.

"No," he said in English. "Enough's enough. Don't break the other one."

Pickering looked disappointed, but he let Ahruntinok's arm drop, and stepped back. The giant lay huddled face down on the hard snow, still conscious but not moving. His great body was racked by three loud, bitter, bewildered sobs. He made no attempt to rise.

—the harder they fall, Norden thought.

Pickering was coming off the battlefield now. He was gasping hard for breath, and his skin was blue and goose-pimpled from the cold, but he was traveling under his own steam. He crossed the field, drew near the Overman and the Grand Judge, and sank to the ground at their feet.

Kneeling, he looked up at the Overman and repeated the words Norden had taught him.

114

Precedent

"My lord, I ask forgiveness for what I've done. The guilt of blasphemy lies on me still. Will you deign to punish me?"

If Pickering had struck him in the face, the Overman could not have looked more astonished. Mouth open, he stared from the huddled figure of Ahruntinok lying alone in the center of the gaming-ground to the kneeling figure of Pickering. In a hesitant, surprisingly small voice he said, "Punish you? The trial is over, and you have won. How can we punish you now?"

"I insist, my lord. I blasphemed at your temple."

Norden forced back a grin at the Overman's discomfiture. The priest-king was looking at the Grand Judge as if expecting some answer, some way out of this dilemma: how could Pickering have committed blasphemy if the result of the trial-by-combat showed clearly he was innocent? There had been a hundred witnesses to his act. How—?

The Grand Judge, of course, had no answer.

Norden stepped forward. It was not part of his plan to humiliate the Overman before all his village.

He said, "The man is clearly innocent by your law. I ask your permission to take him back, to settle his case among ourselves. May we have him? Will you release him from your custody?"

Something similar to horror passed over the Overman's face. "Yes," he said, much too quickly. "The man's yours. The matter's ended, so far as we're concerned. Take him! Take him!"

But the matter, of course, was far from ended so far as the Leeminorrans were concerned. Their troubles, Norden thought, were just beginning.

He stared at the solidophoned figure of Director Thornton and said, "I did the same thing Devall did, sir. One of my men committed a crime against their laws, they came to me to demand him for trial, and I handed him over to them. You have to admit I was perfectly fairminded about it."

"You were," Thornton chuckled. "Clean and aboveboard in the dirtiest way possible."

"I object! Just because I handpicked my criminal, and just because he *deliberately* committed blasphemy in the most open and casual manner, and just because I knew that Leeminorran law provided recourse to trial by combat if the accused man requested it—"

"—and just because your man Pickering just happened to be one of Earth's most murderous professional boxers," Thornton added—

"Well? The job got done, didn't it?" Norden demanded.

"It did indeed. And very well, too, according to your report. There'll be a commendation for you, Norden. And when you're through with Leeminorr, I'll try to find a less wintry world for your next stop. Seems to me you've had a succession of rough assignments."

"I like it that way, sir," Norden said quietly.

"But—"

"Sir?"

That was all he needed to say.

Later, as he sat alone in his room filling out the routine report on the weather for that day, he paused to think over what he had done.

He felt pretty good about it. He had come to Leeminorr with a purpose, and he had fulfilled that purpose.

He scribbled busily away. *Fifth September 2709. Colonel*

Precedent

Lorne Norden reporting. Eighteenth day of our stay on Leeminorr, World Five of System 2279-sub-c. Morning temperature 23 at 0700.—

The Corps, he thought, had been saddled by the Devall Precedent: when an Earthman commits a crime on an alien world where he's part of a study team, he's responsible to the inhabitants of that world.

Devall had been an intelligent man, but a fuzzy thinker. His line of reasoning was down in his report: *I believed I should treat the aliens as equals, and the best way to prove this equality to them was to subject ourselves to their legal code.*

That was all well and good, thought Norden, as he continued working. There was only one minor hitch: the aliens were *not* equal. It was sloppy-minded to insist that they were.

The Markins had used trial by ordeal; the Leeminorrans, trial by combat. Both good systems, in their day—but not the best. Their results had little to do with actual justice, much as their proponents thought they did.

Norden had fought a double battle, and had won both. He had effectively smashed the Devall Precedent, and he had taught the Leeminorrans a few things about justice.

Simple. Just see to it that your man commits a flagrant abuse of the law in the presence of a few hundred witnesses —and then, when they take him away for trial, have him prove his undeniable innocence *by their laws*. Then let them square the problem of how a man can so obviously commit blasphemy and still get away with it at trial.

That ought to shake a couple of their concepts, Norden thought. It ought to show them a thing or two about the

117

effectiveness of trial by combat. And they'll think twice before they hail an Earthman up before their courts again, too.

He finished writing, closed up, and filed away the log. He walked to the window. Night had fallen; the splinter of moon was overhead, and a light snow was dropping through the cold darkness.

Devall's mistake had been to treat his bunch of aliens as if they were equals, when they really weren't—not *yet*. Norden had shown the Leeminorrans the flaw in the Devall Precedent: if you want to be treated like equals, you have to face the consequences. And the consequences, in this case, proved pretty ugly for poor Ahruntinok.

But he'd recover, and the Leeminorrans would learn something from the incident. Norden smiled.

He liked the sound of it: Norden's Precedent. *If aliens demand equality with Earthmen, give 'em all the equality they can stand. Give it to 'em till it hurts!*

That would hold as a good rule of thumb, Norden thought. Until the race came along that really *deserved* equality, and that was a different matter.

He snapped off the light and headed out into the snow, trotting across the compound to the medical building. The docs were fixing up Pickering, taking the bruises out of him and removing the dent a wild swipe had put in his nose. Pickering had gone through a lot lately, Norden thought. The Colonel wanted to congratulate him for a good job, well done.

Mugwump 4

Al Miller was only trying to phone the Friendly Finance Corporation to ask about an extension on his loan. It was a Murray Hill number, and he had dialed as far as MU-4 when the receiver clicked queerly and a voice said, "Come in, Operator Nine. Operator Nine, do you read me?"

Al frowned. "I didn't want the operator. There must be something wrong with my phone if—"

"Just a minute. Who *are* you?"

"I ought to ask *you* that," Al said. "What are you doing on the other end of my phone, anyway? I hadn't even finished dialing. I got as far as MU-4 and—"

"Well? You dialed MUgwump 4 and you got us. What more do you want?" A suspicious pause. "Say, you aren't Operator Nine!"

"No, I'm *not* Operator Nine, and I'm trying to dial a Murray Hill number, and how about getting off the line?"

"Hold it, friend. Are you a Normal?"

Al blinked. "Yeah—yeah, I like to think so."

"So how'd you know the Number?"

"Dammit, I *didn't* know the number! I was trying to call someone, and all of a sudden the phone cut out and I got you, whoever the blazes *you* are."

"I'm the communications warden at MUgwump 4," the other said crisply. "And you're a suspicious individual. We'll have to investigate you."

The telephone emitted a sudden burping sound. Al felt as if his feet had grown roots. He could not move at all. It was awkward to be standing there at his own telephone in the privacy of his own room, as unbending as the Apollo Belvedere. Time still moved, he saw. The hand on the big clock above the phone had just shifted from 3:30 to 3:31.

Sweat rivered down his back as he struggled to put down the phone. He fought to lift his left foot. He strained to twitch his right eyelid. No go on all counts; he was frozen, all but his chest muscles—thank goodness for that. He still could breathe.

A few minutes later matters became even more awkward when his front door, which had been locked, opened abruptly. Three strangers entered. They looked oddly alike: a trio of Tweedledums, no more than five feet high, each wide through the waist, jowly of face and balding of head, each wearing an inadequate single-breasted blue-serge suit.

Al discovered he could roll his eyes. He rolled them. He wanted to apologize because his unexpected paralysis kept him from acting the proper part of a host, but his tongue would not obey. And on second thought, it occurred that the little bald men might be connected in some way with that paralysis.

The reddest-faced of the three little men made an intricate gesture and the stasis ended. Al nearly folded up as the tension that gripped him broke. He said, "Just who the deuce—"

"*We* will ask the questions. You are Al Miller?"

Al nodded.

"And obviously you are a Normal. So there has been a grave error. Mordecai, examine the telephone."

The second little man picked up the phone and calmly disemboweled it with three involved motions of his stubby hands. He frowned over the telephone's innards for a moment; then, humming tunelessly, he produced a wire-clipper and severed the telephone cord.

"Hold on here," Al burst out. "You can't just rip out my phone like that! You aren't from the phone company!"

"Quiet," said the spokesman nastily. "Well, Mordecai?"

The second little man said, "Probability 1:1,000,000. The cranch interval overlapped and his telephone matrix slipped. His call was piped into our wire by error, Waldemar."

"So he isn't a spy?" Waldemar asked.

"Doubtful. As you see, he's of rudimentary intelligence. His dialing our number was a statistical fluke."

"But now he knows about Us," said the third little man in a surprisingly deep voice. "I vote for demolecularization."

The other two whirled on their companion. "Always bloodthirsty, eh, Giovanni?" said Mordecai. "You'd violate the Code at the snap of a meson."

"There won't be any demolecularization while *I'm* in charge," added Waldemar.

"What do we do with him, then?" Giovanni demanded.

Mordecai said, "Freeze him and take him down to Head-quarters. He's *their* problem."

"I think this has gone about as far as it's going to go," Al exploded at last. "However you three creeps got in here, you'd better get yourselves right out again, or—"

"Enough," Waldemar said. He stamped his foot. Al felt his jaws stiffen. He realized bewilderedly that he was frozen again. And frozen, this time, with his mouth gaping fool-ishly open.

The trip took about five minutes, and so far as Al was concerned it was one long blur. At the end of the journey the blur lifted for an instant, just enough to give Al one good glimpse of his surroundings—a residential street in what might have been Brooklyn or Queens (or Cincinnati or Detroit, he thought morbidly)—before he was hustled into the basement of a two-family house. He found himself in a windowless, brightly lit chamber cluttered with com-plex-looking machinery and with a dozen or so alarmingly identical little bald-headed men.

The chubbiest of the bunch glared sourly at him and asked, "Are you a spy?"

"I'm just an innocent bystander. I picked up my phone and started to dial, and all of a sudden some guy asked me if I was Operator Nine. Honest, that's all."

"Overlapping of the cranch interval," muttered Morde-cai. "Slipped matrix."

"Umm. Unfortunate," the chubby one commented. "We'll have to dispose of him."

"Demolecularization is the best way," Giovanni put in immediately.

Mugwump 4

"Dispose of him *humanely,* I mean. It's revolting to think of taking the life of an inferior being. But he simply can't remain in this fourspace any longer, not if he Knows."

"But I *don't* know!" Al groaned. "I couldn't be any more mixed-up if I tried! Won't you please tell me—"

"Very well," said the pudgiest one, who seemed to be the leader. "Waldemar, tell him about Us."

Waldemar said, "You're now in the local headquarters of a secret mutant group working for the overthrow of humanity as you know it. By some accident you happened to dial our private communication exchange, MUtant 4—"

"I thought it was MUgwump 4," Al interjected.

"The code name, naturally," said Waldemar smoothly. "To continue: you channelled into our communication network. You now know too much. Your presence in this space-time nexus jeopardizes the success of our entire movement. Therefore we are forced—"

"To demolecularize—" Giovanni began.

"Forced to dispose of you," Waldemar continued sternly. "We're humane beings—most of us—and we won't do anything that would make you suffer. But you can't stay in this area of space-time. You see our point of view, of course."

Al shook his head dimly. These little potbellied men were mutants working for the overthrow of humanity? Well, he had no reason to think they were lying to him. The world was full of little potbellied men. Maybe they were all part of the secret organization, Al thought.

"Look," he said, "I didn't *want* to dial your number, get me? It was all a big accident. But I'm a fair guy. Let me get out of here and I'll keep mum about the whole thing.

You can go ahead and overthrow humanity, if that's what you want to do. I promise not to interfere in any way. If you're mutants, you ought to be able to look into my mind and see that I'm sincere—"

"We have no telepathic powers," declared the chubby leader curtly. "If we had, there would be no need for a communications network in the first place. In the second place, your sincerity is not the issue. We have enemies. If you were to fall into their hands—"

"I won't say a word! Even if they stick splinters under my fingernails, I'll keep quiet!"

"No. At this stage in our campaign we can take no risks. You'll have to go. Prepare the temporal centrifuge."

Four of the little men, led by Mordecai, unveiled a complicated-looking device of the general size and shape of a concrete mixer. Waldemar and Giovanni gently shoved Al toward the machine. It came rapidly to life: dials glowed, indicator needles teetered, loud buzzes and clicks implied readiness.

Al said nervously, "What are you going to do to me?"

Waldemar explained. "This machine will hurl you forward in time. Too bad we have to rip you right out of your temporal matrix, but we've no choice. You'll be well taken care of up ahead, though. No doubt by the Twenty-fifth Century our kind will have taken over completely. You'll be the last of the Normals. Practically a living fossil. You'll love it. You'll be a walking museum piece."

"Assuming the machine works," Giovanni put in maliciously. "We don't really know if it does, you see."

Al gaped. They were busily strapping him to a cold copper slab in the heart of the machine. "You don't even know if it *works?*"

"Not really," Waldemar admitted. "Present theory holds that time-travel works only one way—*forward*. So we haven't been able to recover any of our test specimens and see how they reacted. Of course, they *do* vanish when the machine is turned on, so we know they must go *somewhere*."

"Oh," Al said weakly.

He was trussed in thoroughly. Experimental wriggling of his right wrist showed him that. But even if he could get loose, these weird little men would only "freeze" him and put him into the machine again.

His shoulders slumped resignedly. He wondered if anyone would miss him. The Friendly Finance Corporation certainly would. But since, in a sense, it was their fault he was in this mess now, he couldn't get very upset about that. They could always sue his estate for the $300 he owed them, if his estate were worth that much.

Nobody else was going to mind the disappearance of Albert Miller from the space-time continuum, he thought dourly. His parents were dead, he hadn't seen his one sister in fifteen years, and the girl he used to know in Topeka was married and at last report had three kids.

Still and all, he rather liked 1969. He wasn't sure how he would take to the Twenty-fifth Century—or the Twenty-fifth Century to him.

"Ready for temporal discharge," Mordecai sang out.

The chubby leader peered up at Al. "We're sorry about all this, you understand. But nothing and nobody can be allowed to stand in the way of the Cause."

"Sure," Al said. "I understand."

The concrete-mixer part of the machine began to revolve, bearing Al with it as it built up tempokinetic potential. Momentum increased alarmingly. In the background Al heard an ominous droning sound that grew louder and louder, until it drowned out everything else. His head reeled. The room and its fat little mutants went blurry. He heard a *pop!* like the sound of a breaking balloon.

It was the rupturing of the space-time continuum. Al Miller went hurtling forward along the fourspace track, head first. He shut his eyes and hoped for the best.

When the dizziness stopped, he found himself sitting in the middle of an impeccably clean, faintly yielding roadway, staring up at the wheels of vehicles swishing by overhead at phenomenal speeds. After a moment or two more, he realized they were not airborne, but simply automobiles racing along an elevated roadway made of some practically invisible substance.

So the temporal centrifuge *had* worked! Al glanced around. A crowd was collecting. A couple of hundred people had formed a big circle. They were pointing and muttering. Nobody approached closer than fifty or sixty feet.

They weren't potbellied mutants. Without exception they were all straight-backed six-footers with full heads of hair. The women were tall, too. Men and women alike were dressed in a sort of tunic-like garment made of iridescent material that constantly changed colors.

A gong began to ring, rapidly peaking in volume. Al scrambled to his feet and assayed a tentative smile.

"My name's Miller. I come from 1969. Would somebody mind telling me what year this is, and—"

He was drowned out by two hundred voices screaming in terror. The crowd stampeded away, dashing madly in every direction, as if he were some ferocious monster. The gong continued to clang loudly. Cars hummed overhead. Suddenly Al saw a squat, beetle-shaped black vehicle coming toward him on the otherwise empty road. The car pulled up half a block away, the top sprang open, and a figure clad in what might have been a diver's suit—or a spacesuit —stepped out and advanced toward Al.

"Dozzinon murrifar volan," the armored figure called out.

"No speaka da lingo," Al replied. "I'm a stranger here."

To his dismay he saw the other draw something shaped like a weapon and point it at him. Al's hands shot immediately into the air. A globe of bluish light exuded from the broad nozzle of the gun, hung suspended for a moment, and drifted toward Al. He dodged uneasily to one side, but the globe of light followed him, descended, and wrapped itself completely around him.

It was like being on the inside of a soap-bubble. He could see out, though distortedly. He touched the curving side of the globe experimentally; it was resilient and springy to the touch, but his finger did not penetrate.

He noticed with some misgiving that his bubble-cage was starting to drift off the ground. It trailed a rope-like extension, which the man in the spacesuit deftly grabbed and knotted to the rear bumper of his car. He drove quickly away—with Al, bobbing in his impenetrable bubble of light, tagging willy-nilly along like a caged tiger, or like a captured Gaul being dragged through the streets of Rome behind a chariot.

He got used to the irregular motion after a while, and relaxed enough to be able to study his surroundings. He was passing through a remarkably antiseptic-looking city, free from refuse and dust. Towering buildings, all bright and spankingly new-looking, shot up everywhere. People goggled at him from the safety of the pedestrian walkways as he jounced past.

After about ten minutes the car halted outside an imposing building whose facade bore the words ISTFAQ BARNOLL. Three men in spacesuits appeared from within to flank Al's captor as a kind of honor guard. Al was borne within.

He was nudged gently into a small room on the ground floor. The door rolled shut behind him and seemed to join the rest of the wall; no division line was apparent. A moment later the balloon popped open, and just in time, too; the air had been getting quite stale inside it.

Al glanced around. A square window opened in the wall and three grim-faced men peered intently at him from an adjoining cubicle. A voice from a speaker grid above Al's head said, "Murrifar althrosk?"

"Al Miller, from the twentieth century. And it wasn't my idea to come here, believe me."

"Durberal haznik? Quittimar? Dorbfenk?"

Al shrugged. "No parley-voo. Honest, I don't savvy."

His three interrogators conferred among themselves—taking what seemed to Al like the needless precaution of switching off the mike to prevent him from overhearing their deliberations. He saw one of the men leave the observation cubicle. When he returned, some five minutes later, he brought with him a tall, gloomy-looking man wearing an impressive spade-shaped beard.

The mike was turned on again. Spadebeard said rumblingly, "How be thou hight?"

"Eh?"

"An thou reck the King's tongue, I conjure thee speak!"

Al grinned. No doubt they had fetched an expert in ancient languages to talk to him. "Right language, but the wrong time. I'm from the *twentieth* century. Come forward a ways."

Spadebeard paused to change mental gears. "A thousand pardons—I mean, *sorry*. Wrong idiom. Dig me now?"

"I follow you. What year is this?"

"2431. And from whence be you?"

"You don't quite have it straight, yet. But I'm from 1969."

"And how came you hither?"

"I wish I knew," Al said. "I was just trying to phone the loan company, see . . . anyway, I got involved with these little fat guys who wanted to take over the world. Mutants, they said they were. And they decided they had to get rid of me, so they bundled me into their time machine and shot me forward. So I'm here."

"A spy of the mutated ones, eh?"

"Spy? Who said anything about being a spy? Talk about jumping to conclusions! I'm—"

"You have been sent by Them to wreak mischief among us. No transparent story of yours will deceive us. You are not the first to come to our era, you know. And you will meet the same fate the others met."

Al shook his head foggily. "Look here, you're making some big mistake. I'm not a spy for anybody. And I don't want to get involved in any war between you and the mutants—"

"The war is over. The last of the mutated ones was exterminated fifty years ago."

129

"Okay, then. What can you fear from me? Honest, I don't want to cause any trouble. If the mutants are wiped out, how could my spying help them?"

"No action in time and space is ever absolute. In our fourspace the mutants are eradicated—but they lurk elsewhere, waiting for their chance to enter and spread destruction."

Al's brain was swimming. "Okay, let that pass. But I'm *not* a spy. I just want to be left alone. Let me settle down here somewhere—put me on probation—show me the ropes, stake me to a few credits, or whatever you use for money here. I won't make any trouble."

"Your body teems with microorganisms of disease long since extinct in this world. Only the fact that we were able to confine you in a force-bubble almost as soon as you arrived here saved us from a terrible epidemic of ancient diseases."

"A couple of injections, that's all, and you can kill any bacteria on me," Al pleaded. "You're advanced people. You ought to be able to do a simple thing like that."

"And then there is the matter of your genetic structure," Spadebeard continued inexorably. "You bear genes long since eliminated from humanity as undesirable. Permitting you to remain here, breeding uncontrollably, would introduce unutterable confusion. Perhaps you carry latently the same mutant strain that cost humanity so many centuries of bloodshed!"

"No," Al protested. "Look at me. I'm six feet tall, no potbelly, a full head of hair—"

"The gene is recessive. But it crops up unexpectedly."

"I solemnly promise to control my breeding," Al declared. "I won't run around scattering my genes all over your shiny new world. That's a promise."

"Your appeal is rejected," came the inflexible reply.

Al shrugged. He knew when he was beaten. "Okay," he said wearily. "I didn't want to live in your damn century anyway. When's the execution?"

"*Execution?*" Spadebeard looked stunned. "The Twentieth-Century referent—yes, it is! Dove's whiskers, do you think we would—would actually—"

He couldn't get the word out. Al supplied it.

"Put me to death?"

Spadebeard's expression was sickly. He looked ready to retch. Al heard him mutter vehemently to his companions in the observation cubicle: "Gonnim def larrimog! Egfar!"

"Murrifar althrosk," suggested one of his companions.

Spadebeard, evidently reassured, nodded. He said to Al, "No doubt a barbarian like yourself *would* expect to be— to be made dead." Gulping, he went gamely on. "We have no such vindictive intention."

"Well, what *are* you going to do to me?"

"Send you across the timeline to a world where your friends the mutated ones reign supreme," Spadebeard replied. "It's the least we can do for you, spy."

The hidden door of his cell puckered open. Another space-suited figure entered, pointed a gun, and discharged a blob of blue light that drifted toward Al and rapidly englobed him. He was drawn by the trailing end out into a corridor.

It hadn't been a very sociable reception, here in the Twenty-fifth Century, he thought as he was tugged along the hallway. In a way, he couldn't blame them. A time-traveler from the past was bound to be laden down with all sorts of germs. They couldn't risk letting him running around *breathing* at everybody. No wonder that crowd of onlookers had panicked when he opened his mouth to speak to them.

The other business, though, that of his being a spy for the mutants—he couldn't figure that out at all. If the mutants had been wiped out fifty years ago, why worry about spies now? At least his species had managed to defeat the underground organization of potbellied little men. That was comforting. He wished he could get back to 1969 if only to snap his fingers in their jowly faces and tell them that all their sinister scheming was going to come to nothing.

Where was he heading now? Spadebeard had said, *Across the timeline to a world where the mutated ones reign supreme.* Whatever across the timeline meant, Al thought.

He was ushered into an impressive laboratory room and, bubble and all, was thrust into the waiting clasps of something that looked depressingly like an electric chair. Brisk technicians bustled around, throwing switches and checking connections.

Al glanced appealingly at Spadebeard. "Will you tell me what's going on?"

"It is very difficult to express it in medieval terms," the linguist said. "The device makes use of dollibar force to transmit you through an inverse dormin vector—do I make myself clear?"

"Not very."

"Unhelpable. But you understand the concept of parallel continua at least, of course."

"No."

"Does it mean anything to you if I say that you'll be shunted across the spokes of the time-wheel to a totality that is simultaneously parallel and tangent to our four-space?"

"I get the general idea," Al said dubiously, though all he was really getting was a headache. "You might as well start shunting me, I suppose."

Spadebeard nodded and turned to a technician. "Vorstrar althrosk," he commanded.

"Murrifar."

The technician grabbed an immense toggle switch with both hands and groaningly dragged it shut. Al heard a brief whine of closing relays. Then darkness surrounded him.

Once again he found himself on a city street. But the pavement was cracked and buckled, and grass-blades shot up through the neglected concrete.

A dry voice said, "All right, you. Don't sprawl there like a ninny. Get up and come along."

Al peered doubtfully up into the snout of a fair-sized pistol of enormous caliber. It was held by a short, fat, bald-headed man. Four identical companions stood near him with arms folded. They all looked very much like Mordecai, Waldemar, Giovanni, and the rest, except that these mutants were decked out in futuristic-looking costumes bright with flashy gold trim and rocketship insignia.

Al put up his hands. "Where am I?" he asked hesitantly.

"Earth, of course. You've just come through a dimensional gateway from the continuum of the Normals. Come along, spy. Into the van."

"But I'm *not* a spy," Al mumbled protestingly, as the five little men bundled him into a blue and red car the size of a small yacht. "At least, I'm not spying on *you*. I mean—"

"Save the explanations for the Overlord," was the curt instruction.

Al huddled miserably cramped between two vigilant mutants, while the others sat behind him. The van moved seemingly of its own volition, and at an enormous rate. A mutant power, Al thought. After a while he said, "Could you at least tell me what year this is?"

"2431," snapped the mutant to his left.

"But that's the same year it was over *there*."

"Of course. What did you expect?"

The question floored Al. He was silent for perhaps half a mile more. Since the van had no windows, he stared morosely at his feet. Finally he asked, "How come you aren't afraid of catching my germs, then? Over back of— ah—the dimensional gateway, they kept me cooped up in a force-field all the time so I wouldn't contaminate them. But you go right ahead breathing the same air I do."

"Do you think we fear the germs of a Normal, spy?" sneered the mutant at Al's right. "You forget that we're a superior race."

Al nodded. "Yes. I forgot about that."

The van halted suddenly and the mutant police hustled Al out, past a crowd of peering little fat men and women, and into a colossal dome of a building whose exterior was covered completely with faceted green glass. The effect was one of massive ugliness.

They ushered him into a sort of throne room presided over by a mutant fatter than the rest. The policeman gripping Al's right arm hissed, "Bow when you enter the presence of the Overlord."

Al wasn't minded to argue. He dropped to his knees along with the others. A booming voice from above rang out. "What have you brought me today?"

"A spy, your nobility."

"Another? Rise, spy."

Al rose. "Begging your nobility's pardon, I'd like to put in a word or two on my own behalf—"

"Silence!" the Overlord roared.

Al closed his mouth. The mutant drew himself up to his full height, about five feet one, and said, "The Normals have sent you across the dimensional gulf to spy on us."

"No, your nobility. They were afraid I'd spy on *them,* so they tossed me over here. I'm from the year 1969, you see." Briefly, he explained everything, beginning with the bollixed phone call and ending with his capture by the Overlord's men a short while ago.

The Overlord looked skeptical. "It is well known that the Normals plan to cross the dimensional gulf from their phantom world to this, the real one, and invade our civilization. You're but the latest of their advance scouts. Admit it!"

"Sorry, your nobility, but I'm not. On the other side they told me I was a spy from 1969, and now you say I'm a spy from the other dimension. But I tell you—"

"Enough!" the mutant leader thundered. "Take him away. Place him in custody. We shall decide his fate later!"

Someone else already occupied the cell into which Al was thrust. He was a lanky, sad-faced Normal who slouched forward to shake hands once the door had clanged shut.

"Thurizad manifosk," he said.

"Sorry. I don't speak that language," said Al.

The other grinned. "I understand. All right: greetings. I'm Darren Phelp. Are you a spy too?"

"No, dammit!" Al snapped. Then: "Sorry. Didn't mean to take it out on you. My name's Al Miller. Are you a native of this place?"

"Me? Dove's whiskers, what a sense of humor! Of course I'm not a native! You know as well as I do that there aren't any Normals left in this fourspace continuum."

"None at all?"

"Hasn't been one born here in centuries," Phelp said. "But you're just joking, eh? You're from Baileffod's outfit, I suppose."

"Who?"

"Baileffod. *Baileffod!* You mean you aren't? Then you must be from Higher Up!" Phelp thrust his hands sideways in some kind of gesture of respect. "Penguin's paws, Excellency, I apologize. I should have seen at once—"

"No, I'm not from your organization at all," Al said. "I don't know what you're talking about, really."

Phelp smiled cunningly. "Of *course,* Excellency! I understand completely."

"Cut that out! Why doesn't anyone ever believe me? I'm not from Baileffod and I'm not from Higher Up. I come from 1969. Do you hear me, 1969? And that's the truth."

Phelp's eyes went wide. "From the *past?*"

Al nodded. "I stumbled into the mutants in 1969 and they threw me five centuries ahead to get rid of me. Only when I arrived, I wasn't welcome, so I was shipped across the dimensional whatzis to here. Everyone thinks I'm a spy, wherever I go. What are *you* doing here?"

Phelp smiled. "Why, I *am* a spy."

"From 2431?"

"Naturally. We have to keep tabs on the mutants some-how. I came through the gateway wearing an invisibility shield, but it popped an ultrone and I vizzed out. They jugged me last month, and I suppose I'm here for keeps."

Al rubbed thumbs tiredly against his eyeballs. "Wait a minute—how come you speak my language? On the other side they had to get a linguistics expert to talk to me."

"All spies are trained to talk English, stupid. That's the language the mutants speak here. In the real world we speak Vorkish, naturally. It's the language developed by Normals for communication during the Mutant Wars. Your 'linguistics expert' was probably one of our top spies."

"And over here the mutants have won?"

"Completely. Three hundred years ago, in this continuum, the mutants developed a two-way time machine that enabled them to go back and forth, eliminating Normal leaders before they were born. Whereas in our world, the *real* world, two-way time travel is impossible. That's where the continuum split begins. We Normals fought a grim war of extermination against the mutants in our fourspace and finally wiped them out, despite their superior mental powers, in 2390. Clear?"

"More or less." Rather less than more, Al added privately. "So there are only mutants in this world, and only Normals in your world."

"Exactly!"

"And you're a spy from the other side."

"You've got it now! You see, even though strictly speaking this world is only a phantom, it's got some pretty real characteristics. For instance, if the mutants killed you here, you'd be dead. Permanently. So there's a lot of rivalry across the gateway; the mutants are always scheming to invade us, and vice versa. Confidentially, I don't think anything will ever come of all the scheming."

"You don't?"

"Nah," Phelp said. "The way things stand now, each side has a perfectly good enemy just beyond reach. But actually going to war would be messy, while relaxing our guard and slipping into peace would foul up our economy. So we keep sending spies back and forth, and prepare for war. It's a nice system, except when you happen to get caught, like me."

"What'll happen to you?"

Phelp shrugged. "They may let me rot here for a few decades. Or they might decide to condition me and send me back as a spy for *them*. Tiger tails, who knows?"

"Would you change sides like that?"

"I wouldn't have any choice—not after I was conditioned," Phelp said. "But I don't worry much about it. It's a risk I knew about when I signed on for spy duty."

Al shuddered. It was beyond him how someone could *voluntarily* let himself get involved in this game of dimension-shifting and mutant-battling. But it takes all sorts to make a continuum, he decided.

Half an hour later three rotund mutant police came to fetch him. They marched him downstairs and into a bare, ugly little room where a battery of interrogators quizzed him for better than an hour. He stuck to his story, throughout everything, until at last they indicated they were through with him. He spent the next two hours in a drafty cell, by himself, until finally a gaudily-robed mutant unlocked the door and said, "The Overlord wishes to see you."

The Overlord looked worried. He leaned forward on his throne, fist digging into his fleshy chin. In his booming voice—Al realized suddenly that it was artificially amplified—the Overlord rumbled, "Miller, you're a *problem*."

"I'm sorry, your nobil—"

"*Quiet!* I'll do the talking."

Al did not reply.

The Overlord went on, "We've checked your story inside and out, and confirmed it with one of our spies on the other side of the gate. You really *are* from 1969, or thereabouts. What can we do with you? Generally speaking, when we catch a Normal snooping around here, we psychocondition him and send him back across the gateway to spy for us. But we can't do that to you, because you don't belong on the other side, and they've already tossed you out once. On the other hand, we can't keep you here, maintaining you forever at state expense. And it wouldn't be civilized to kill you, would it?"

"No, your nobil—"

"*Silence!*"

Al gulped. The Overlord glowered at him and continued thinking out loud. "I suppose we could perform experiments on you, though. You must be a walking laboratory of Normal microorganisms that we could synthesize and fire through the gateway when we invade their fourspace. Yes, by the Grome, then you'd be useful to our cause! Zechariah?"

"Yes, Nobility?" A ribbon-bedecked guardsman snapped to attention.

"Take this Normal to the Biological Laboratories for

examination. I'll have further instructions as soon as—"

Al heard a peculiar whanging noise from the back of the throne room. The Overlord appeared to freeze on his throne. Turning, Al saw a band of determined-looking Normals come bursting in, led by Darren Phelp.

"*There* you are!" Phelp cried. "I've been looking all over for you!" He was waving a peculiar needle-nozzled gun.

"What's going on?" Al asked.

Phelp grinned. "The Invasion! It came, after all! Our troops are pouring through the gateway armed with these freezer guns. They immobilize any mutant who gets in the way of the field."

"When—when did all this happen?"

"It started two hours ago. We've captured the entire city! Come on, will you? Whiskers, there's no time to waste!"

"Where am I supposed to go?"

Phelp smiled. "To the nearest dimensional lab, of course. We're going to send you back home."

A dozen triumphant Normals stood in a tense knot around Al in the laboratory. From outside came the sound of jubilant singing. The Invasion was a howling success.

As Phelp had explained it, the victory was due to the recent invention of a kind of time-barrier projector. The projector had cut off all contact between the mutant world and its own future, preventing time-travelling mutant scouts from getting back to 2431 with news of the Invasion. Thus two-way travel, the great mutant advantage, was nullified, and the success of the surprise attack was made possible.

Al listened to this explanation with minimal interest. He

barely understood every third word, and, in any event, his main concern was in getting home.

He was strapped into a streamlined and much modified version of the temporal centrifuge that had originally hurled him into 2431. Phelp explained things to him.

"You see here, we set the machine for 1969. What day was it when you left?"

"Ah—October 10. Around 3:30 in the afternoon."

"Make the setting, Frozz." Phelp nodded. "You'll be shunted back along the time-line. Of course, you'll land in this continuum, since in our world there's no such thing as pastward time travel. But once you reach your own time, all you do is activate this small transdimensional generator, and you'll be hurled across safe and sound into the very day you left, in your own fourspace."

"You can't know how much I appreciate all this," Al said warmly. He felt a pleasant glow of love for all mankind, for the first time since his unhappy phone call. At last someone was taking sympathetic interest in his plight. At last, he was on his way home, back to the relative sanity of 1969 where he could start forgetting this entire nightmarish jaunt. Mutants and Normals and spies and time machines—

"You'd better get going," Phelp said. "We have to get the occupation under way here."

"Sure," Al agreed. "Don't let me hold you up. I can't wait to get going—no offense intended."

"And remember—soon as your surroundings look familiar, jab the activator button on this generator. Otherwise you'll slither into an interspace where we couldn't answer for the consequences."

Al nodded tensely. "I won't forget."

"I hope not. Ready?"

"Ready."

Someone threw a switch. Al began to spin. He heard the popping sound that was the rupturing of the temporal matrix. Like a cork shot from a champagne bottle, Al arched out backward through time, heading for 1969.

He woke in his own room on 23rd Street. His head hurt. His mind was full of phrases like temporal centrifuge and transdimensional generator.

He picked himself off the floor and rubbed his head.

Wow, he thought. It must have been a sudden fainting spell. And now his head was full of nonsense.

Going to the sideboard, he pulled out the half-empty bourbon bottle and measured off a few fingers' worth. After the drink, his nerves felt steadier. His mind was still cluttered with inexplicable thoughts and images. Sinister little fat men and complex machines, gleaming roadways and men in fancy tunics.

A bad dream, he thought.

Then he remembered. It wasn't any dream. He had actually taken the round trip into 2431, returning by way of some other continuum. He had pressed the generator button at the proper time, and now here he was, safe and sound. No longer the football of a bunch of different factions. Home in his own snug little fourspace, or whatever it was.

He frowned. He recalled that Mordecai had severed the telephone wire. But the phone looked intact now. Maybe it had been fixed while he was gone. He picked it up. Unless he got that loan extension today, he was cooked.

142

Mugwump 4

There was no need for him to look up the number of the Friendly Finance Corporation; he knew it well enough. He began to dial. MUrray Hill 4—

The receiver clicked queerly. A voice said, "Come in, Operator Nine. Operator Nine, do you read me?"

Al's jaw sagged in horror. This is where I came in, he thought wildly. He struggled to put down the phone. But his muscles would not respond. It would be easier to bend the sun in its orbit than to break the path of the continuum. He heard his own voice say, "I didn't want the operator. There must be something wrong with my phone if—"

"Just a minute. Who *are* you?"

Al fought to break the contact. But he was hemmed away in a small corner of his mind while his voice went on, "I ought to ask *you* that. What are you doing on the other end of my phone, anyway? I hadn't even finished dialing. I got as far as MU-4 and—"

Inwardly Al wanted to scream. No scream would come. In this continuum the past (his future) was immutable. He was caught on the track, and there was no escape. None whatever. And, he realized glumly, there never would be.

Why?

And we left Capella XXII, after a six-month stay, and hopskipped across the galaxy to Dschubba, in the forehead of the Scorpion. And after the eight worlds of Dschubba had been seen and digested and recorded and classified, and after we had programmed all our material for transmission back to Earth, we moved on again, Brock and I.

We zeroed into warp and doublesqueaked into the star Pavo, which from Earth is seen to be the brightest star of the Peacock. And Pavo proved to be planetless, save for one ball of mud and methane a billion miles out; we chalked the mission off as unpromising, and moved on once again.

Brock was the coordinator; I, the fine-tooth man. He saw in patterns; I, in particular. We had been teamed for eleven years. We had visited seventy-eight stars and one hundred sixty-three planets. The end was not quite in sight.

We hung in the grayness of warp, suspended neither in space nor in not-space, hovering in an interstice. Brock said, "I vote for Markab."

144

Why?

"Alpha Pegasi? No. I vote for Etamin."

But Gamma Draconis held little magic for him. He rubbed his angular hands through his tight-cropped hair and said, "The Wheel, then."

I nodded. "The Wheel."

The Wheel was our guide: not really a wheel so much as a map of the heavens in three dimensions, a lens of the galaxy, sprinkled brightly with stars. I pulled a switch; a beam of light lanced down from the ship's wall, needle-thin, playing against the Wheel. Brock seized the handle and imparted axial spin to the Wheel. Over and over for three, four, five rotations; then, stop. The light-beam stung Alphecca.

"Alphecca it will be," Brock said.

"Yes. Alphecca." I noted it in the log, and began setting up the coordinates on the drive. Brock was frowning uneasily.

"This failure to agree," he said. "This inability to decide on a matter so simple as our next destination—"

"Yes. Elucidate. Expound. Exegetise. What pattern do you see in that?"

Scowling he said, "Disagreement for the sake of disagreement is unhealthy. Conflict is valuable, but not for its own sake. It worries me."

"Perhaps we've been in space too long. Perhaps we should resign our commissions, leave the Exploratory Corps, return to Earth and settle there."

His face drained of blood. "No," he said. "No. No."

We emerged from warp within humming-distance of Alphecca, a bright star orbited by four worlds. Brock was playing calculus at the time; driblets of sweat glossed his face at each integration. I peered through the thick quartz of the observation panel and counted planets.

"Four worlds," I said. "One, two, three, and four."

I looked at him. His unfleshy face was tight with pain. After nearly a minute he said, "Pick one."

"Me?"

"*Pick one!*"

"Alphecca II."

"All right. We'll land there. I won't contest the point, Hammond. I *want* to land on Alphecca II." He grinned at me—a bright-eyed wild grin that I found unpleasant. But I saw what he was doing. He was easing a stress-pattern between us, eliminating a source of conflict before the chafing friction exploded. When two men live in a spaceship eleven years, such things are necessary.

Calmly and untensely I took a reading on Alphecca II. I sighted us in and actuated the computer. This was the way a landing was effected; this was the way Brock and I had effected one hundred sixty-three landings. The ion-drive exploded into life.

We dropped "downward." Alphecca II rose to meet us as our slim pale-green needle of a ship dived tail-first toward the world below.

The landing was routine. I sketched out a big 164 on my chart, and we donned spacesuits to make our preliminary explorations. Brock paused a moment at the airlock, smoothing the purple cloth of his suit, adjusting his air-intake, tightening his belt cincture. The corners of his mouth twitched nervously. Within the head-globe he looked frightened, and very tired.

I said, "You're not well. Maybe we should postpone our first look-see."

Why?

"Maybe we should go back to Earth, Hammond. And live in a beehive and breathe filthy gray soup." His voice was edged with bitter reproach. "Let's go outside," he said. He turned away, face shadowed morosely, and touched the stud that peeled back the airlock hatch.

I followed him into the lock and down the elevator. He was silent, stiff, reserved. I wished I had his talent for glimpsing patterns: this mood of his had probably been a long time building.

But I saw no cause for it. After eleven years, I thought, I should know him almost as well as I do myself. Or better. But no easy answers came, and I followed him out onto the exit stage and dropped gently down.

Landing One Six Four was entering the exploratory stage.

The ground spread out far to the horizon, a dull orange in color, rough in texture, pebbly, thick of consistency. We saw a few trees, bare-trunked, bluish. Green vines swarmed over the ground, twisted and gnarled.

Otherwise, nothing.

"Another uninhabited planet," I said. "That makes one hundred eight out of the hundred sixty-four."

"Don't be premature. You can't judge a world by a few acres. Land at a pole; extrapolate utter barrenness. It's not a valid pattern. Not enough evidence."

I cut him short. "Here's one time when I perceive a pattern. I perceive that this world's uninhabited. It's too damned quiet."

Chuckling, Brock said, "I incline to agree. But remember Adhara XI."

I remembered Adhara XI: the small, sandy world far

147

from its primary, which seemed nothing but endless yellow sand dunes, rolling westward round and round the planet. We had joked about the desert-world, dry and parched, inhabited only by the restless dunes. But after the report was written, after our data were codified and flung through subspace toward Earth, we found the oasis on the eastern continent, the tiny garden of green things and sweet air that so sharply was unlike the rest of Adhara XI. I remembered sleek scaly creatures slithering through the crystal lake, and an indolent old worm sleeping beneath a heavy-fruited tree.

"Adhara XI is probably swarming with Earth tourists," I said. "Now that our amended report is public knowledge. I often think we should have concealed the oasis from Earth, and returned there ourselves when we grew tired of exploring the galaxy."

Brock's head snapped up sharply. He ripped a sprouting tip from a leathery vine and said, "*When* we grow tired? Hammond, aren't you tired already? Eleven years, a hundred sixty-four worlds?"

Now I saw the pattern taking fairly clear shape. I shook my head, throttling the conversation. "Let's get down the data, Brock. We can talk later."

We proceeded with the measurements of our particular sector of Alphecca II. We nailed down the dry vital statistics, bracketing them off so Earth could enter the neat figures in its giant catalog of explored worlds.

GRAVITY—*1.02 E.*

ATMOSPHERIC CONSTITUTION—ammonia/carbon dioxide Type ab7, unbreathable

ESTIMATED PLANETARY DIAMETER—.87 E.

INTELLIGENT LIFE—*none*

Why?

We filled out the standard forms, ran the standard tests, took the standard soil samples. Exploration had become a smooth mechanical routine.

Our first tour lasted three hours. We wandered over the slowly rising hills, with the spaceship always at our backs, and Alphecca high behind us. The dry soil crunched unpleasantly beneath our heavy boots.

Conversation was at a minimum. Brock and I rarely spoke when it was not absolutely necessary—and when we did speak, it was to let a tight, tense remark escape confinement, not to communicate anything. We shared too many silent memories. Eleven years and one hundred sixty-four planets. All Brock had to do was say *"Fomalhaut,"* or I *"Theta Eridani,"* and a train of associations and memories was set off in whose depths we could browse silently for hours and hours.

Alphecca II did not promise to be as memorable as those worlds. There would be nothing here to match the fantastic moonrise of Fomalhaut VI, the five hundred mirror-bright moons in stately procession through the sky, each glinting in a different hue. That moonrise had overwhelmed us four years ago, and remained yet bright. Alphecca II, dead world that it was, or rather world not yet alive, would leave no marks on our memories.

But bitterness was rising in Brock. I saw the pattern forming; I saw the question bubbling up through the layers of his mind, ready to be asked.

And on the fourth day, he let it be asked. After four days on Alphecca II, four days of staring at the grotesque twisted green shapes of the angular sprawling vines, four days of watching the lethargic fission of the pond protozoa

149

Why?

who seemed to be the world's only animal life, Brock suddenly looked up at me.

He asked the shattering question that should never be asked.

"Why?" he said.

Eleven years and a hundred sixty-four worlds earlier, the seeds of that unanswered question had been sown. I was fresh out of the Academy, twenty-three, a tall, sharp-nosed boy with what some said was an irritatingly precise way of looking at things.

I should say that I bitterly resented being told I was coldly precise. People accused me of Teutonic heaviness. A girl I once had known said that to me, after a notably unsuccessful romance had come trailing to a halt. I recall turning to her, glaring at the light dusting of freckles across her nose, and telling her, "I have no Teutonic blood whatsoever. If you'll take the trouble to think of the probable Scandinavian derivation of my name—"

She slapped me.

Shortly after that, I met Brock—Brock, who at twenty-four was already the Brock I would know at thirty-five, harsh of face and voice, dark of complexion, with an expression of nervous wariness registering in his blue-black eyes always and ever. Brock never accused me of Teutonicism; he laughed when I cited some minor detail from memory, but the laugh was one of respect.

We were both Academy graduates; we both were restless. It showed in Brock's face, and I don't doubt it showed in mine. Earth was small and dirty and crowded, and each night the stars, those bright enough to glint through the

Why?

haze and brightness of the cities, seemed to mock at us.

Brock and I gravitated naturally together. We shared a room in Appalachia North, we shared a library planchet, we shared reading-tapes and music-disks and occasionally lovers. And eight weeks after my twenty-third birthday, seven weeks before Brock's twenty-fourth, we hailed a cab and invested our last four coins in a trip downtown to the Administration of External Exploration.

There, we spoke to a bland-faced, smiling man with one leg prosthetic—he boasted of it—and his left hand a waxy synthetic one. "I got that way on Sirius VI," he told us. "But I'm an exception. Most of the exploration teams keep going for years and years, and nothing ever happens to them. McKees and Haugmuth have been out twenty-three years now. That's the record. We hear from them, every few months or so. They keep on going, farther and farther out."

Brock nodded. "Good. Give us the forms."

He signed first; I added my name below, finishing with a flourish. I stacked the triplicate forms neatly together and shoved them back at the half-synthetic recruiter.

"Excellent. Excellent. Welcome to the Corps."

He shook our hands, giving the hairy-knuckled right hand to Brock, the waxy left to me. I gripped it tightly, wondering if he could feel my grip.

Three days later we were in space, bound outward. In all the time since the original idea had sprung up unvoiced between us, neither Brock nor myself had paused to ask the damnable question.

Why?

We had joined the Corps. We had renounced Earth.

Why?

Motive, unstated. Or unknown. We let the matter lie dormant between us for eleven years, through a procession of strange and then less strange worlds.

Until Brock's agony broke forth to the surface. He destroyed eleven years of numb peace with one half-whispered syllable, there in the ship's lab our fourth morning on Alphecca II.

I looked at him for perhaps thirty seconds. Moistening my lips, I said, "What do you mean, Brock?"

"You know what I mean." The flat declarative tone was one of simple truth. "The one thing we haven't been asking ourselves all these years, because we knew we didn't have an answer for it and we *like* to have answers for things. Why are we here, on Alphecca II—with a hundred sixty-three visited worlds behind us?"

I shrugged. "You didn't have to start this, Brock." Outside the sun was climbing toward noon height, but I felt cold and dry, as if the ammonia atmosphere were seeping into the ship. It wasn't.

"No," he said. "I didn't have to start this. I could have let it fester for another eleven years. But it came popping out, and I want to settle it. We left Earth because we didn't like it there. Agreed?"

I nodded.

"But that's not *why* enough," he persisted. "Why do we explore? Why do we keep running from planet to planet, from one crazy airless ball to the next, out here where there are no people and no cities? Green crabs on Rigel V, sandfish on Caph. Dammit, Hammond, what are we looking for?"

Very calmly I said, "Ourselves, maybe?"

Why?

His face crinkled scornfully. "Foggy-eyed and imprecise, and you know it. We're not *looking* for ourselves out here. We're trying to *lose* ourselves. Eh?"

"No!"

"Admit it!"

I stared through the quartz window at the stiff, almost wooden vines that covered the pebbly ground. They seemed to be moving faintly, to be stretching their rigid bodies in a contraction of some sort. In a dull, tired voice, Brock said, "We left Earth because we couldn't cope with it. It was too crowded and too dirty for sensitive shrinking souls like us. We had the choice of withdrawing into shells and huddling there for eighty or ninety years, or else pulling up and leaving for space. We left. There's no society out here, just each other."

"We've adjusted to each other," I pointed out.

"So? Does that mean we could fit into Earth society? Would *you* want to go back? Remember the team—McKees and Haugmuth, is it?—who spent thirty-three years in space and came back. They were catatonic eight minutes after landing, the report said."

"Let me give you a simpler *why*," I ventured. "Why did you start griping all of a sudden? Why couldn't you hold it in?"

"That's not a simpler *why*. It's part of the same one. I came to an answer, and I didn't like it. I got the answer that we were out here because we couldn't make the grade on Earth."

"No!"

He smiled apologetically. "No? All right, then. Give me another answer. I *want* an answer, Hammond. I need one, now."

Why?

I pointed to the synthesizer. "Why don't you have a drink instead?"

"That comes later," he said somberly. "After I've given up trying to find out."

The stippling of fine details was becoming a sharp-focus picture. Brock—self-reliant Brock, self-contained, self-sufficient—had come to the end of his self-sufficiency. He had looked too deeply beneath the surface.

"At the age of eight," I began, "I asked my father what was outside the universe. That is, defining the universe as That Which Contains Everything, could there possibly be something or someplace outside its bounds? He looked at me for a minute or two, then laughed and told me not to worry about it. But I did worry about it. I stayed up half the night worrying about it, and my head hurt by morning. I never found out what was outside the universe."

"The universe is infinite," said Brock moodily. "Recurving in on itself, topologically—"

"Maybe. But I worried over it. I worried over First Cause. I worried all through my adolescence. Then I stopped worrying."

He smiled acidly. "You became a vegetable. You rooted yourself in the mud of your own ignorance, and decided not to pull loose because it was too painful. Am I right, Hammond?"

"No. I joined the Exploratory Corps."

I dreamed, that night, as I swung in my hammock. It was a vivid and unpleasant dream, which stayed with me well into the following morning as a sort of misshapen reality that had attached itself to me in the night.

Why?

I had been a long time falling asleep. Brock had brooded most of the day, and a long hike over the bleak tundra had done little to improve his mood. Toward nightfall he dialed a few drinks, inserted a disk of Sibelius in his ear, and sat staring glumly at the darkening sky outside the ship. Alphecca II was moonless. The night was the black of space, but the atmosphere blurred the neighboring stars.

I remember drifting off into a semisleep: a half-somnolence in which I was aware of Brock's harsh breathing to my left, but yet in which I had no volition, no control over my limbs. And after that state came sleep, and with it dreams.

The dream must have grown from Brock's bitter remark of earlier: *You became a vegetable. You rooted yourself in the mud of your own ignorance.*

I accepted the statement literally. Suddenly I *was* a vegetable, possessed of all my former faculties, but rooted in the soil.

Rooted.

Straining for freedom, straining to break away, caught eternally by my legs, thinking, thinking . . .

Never to move, except for a certain thrashing of the upper limbs.

Rooted.

I writhed, longed to get as far as the rocky hill beyond, only as far as the next yard, the next inch. But I had lost all motility. It was as if my legs were grasped in a mighty trap, and, without pain, without torment, I was bound to the earth.

I woke, finally, damp with perspiration. In his hammock, Brock slept, seemingly peacefully. I considered waking him

155

Why?

and telling him of the nightmare, but decided against it. I tried to return to sleep.

At length, I slept.

Dreamlessly.

The preset alarm throbbed at 0700; dawn had preceded us by nearly an hour.

Brock was up first; I sensed him moving about even as I stirred toward wakefulness. Still caught up in the strange unreal reality of my nightmare, I wondered on a conscious level if today would be like yesterday—if Brock, obsessed by his sudden thirst for an answer, would continue to brood and sulk.

I hoped not. It would mean the end of our team if Brock cracked up; after eleven years, I was not anxious for a new partner.

"Hammond? You up yet?"

His voice had lost the edgy quality of yesterday, but there was something new and subliminally frightening in it.

Yawning, I said, "Just about. Dial breakfast for me, will you?"

"I did already. But get out of the sack and come look at this."

I lurched from the hammock, shook my head to clear it, and started forward.

"Where are you?"

"Second level," he said. "At the window. Come take a look."

I climbed the spiral catwalk to the viewing-station; Brock stood with his back toward me, looking out. As I drew near I said, "I had the strangest dream last night—"

Why?

"The hell with that. Look."

At first I didn't notice anything strange. The bright-colored landscape looked unchanged, the pebbly orange soil, the dark blue trees, the tangle of green vines, the murk of the morning atmosphere. But then I saw I had been looking too far from home.

Writhing up the side of the window, just barely visible to the right, was a gnarled knobby green rope. Rope? No. It was one of the vines.

"They're all over the ship," Brock said. "I've checked all the ports. During the night the damned things must have come crawling up the side of the ship like so many snakes and wrapped themselves around us. I guess they figure we're here to stay, and they can use us as bracing-posts the way they do those trees."

I stared with mixed repugnance and fascination at the hard bark of the vine, at the tiny suckers that held it fast to the smooth skin of our ship.

"That's funny," I said. "It's sort of an attack by extraterrestrial monsters, isn't it?"

We suited up and went outside to have a look at the "attackers." At a distance of a hundred yards, the ship looked weirdly bemired. Its graceful lines were broken by the winding fingers of the vine, spiralling up its sleek sides from a thick parent stem on the ground. Other shoots of the vine sprawled near us, clutching futilely at us as we moved among them.

I was reminded of my dream. Somewhat hesitantly I told Brock about it.

He laughed. "Rooted, eh? You were dreaming *that* while

those vines were busy wrapping themselves around the ship. Significant?"

"Perhaps." I eyed the tough vines speculatively. "Maybe we'd better move the ship. If much more of that stuff gets around it, we may not be able to blast off at all."

Brock knelt and flexed a shoot of vine. "The ship could be completely cocooned in this stuff and we'd still be able to take off," he said. "A spacedrive wields a devil of a lot of thrust. We'll manage."

And *whick!*

A tapering finger of the vine arched suddenly and whipped around Brock's middle. *Whick! Whick!*

Like animated rope, like a bark-covered serpent, it curled about him. I drew back, staring. He seemed half amused, half perplexed.

"The thing's got pull, all right," he said. He was smiling lopsidedly, annoyed at having let so simple a thing as a vine interfere with his freedom of motion. But then he winced in obvious pain.

"—Tightening," he gasped.

The vine contracted muscularly; it skittered two or three feet toward the tree from which its parent stock sprang, and Brock was jerked suddenly off balance. As the corded arm of the vine yanked him backward he began to topple, poising for what seemed like seconds on his left foot, right jutting awkwardly in the air, arms clawing for balance.

Then he fell.

I was at his side in a moment, carefully avoiding the innocent-looking vine-tips to right and left. I planted my foot on the trailing vine that held Brock. I levered downward and grabbed the tip where it bound his waist. I pulled; Brock pushed.

Why?

The vine yielded.

"It's giving," he grunted. "A little more."

"Maybe I'd better go back for the blaster," I said.

"No. No telling what this thing may do while you're gone. Cut me in two, maybe. Pull!"

I pulled. The vine struggled against our combined strength, writhed, twisted. But gradually we prevailed. It curled upward, loosened, went limp. Finally it drooped away, leaving Brock in liberty.

He got up slowly, rubbing his waist.

"Hurt?"

"Just the surprise," he said. "Tropistic reaction on the plant's part; I must have triggered some hormone chain to make it do that." He eyed the now quiescent vine with respect.

"It's not the first time we've been attacked," I said. "Alpheraz III—"

"Yes."

I hadn't even needed to mention it. Alpheraz III had been a hellish jungle planet; the image in his mind, as it was in mine, was undoubtedly that of a tawny beast the size of a goat held in the inexorable grip of some stocky-trunked plant, rising in the air, vanishing into a waiting mouth of the carnivorous tree—

—and moments later a second tendril dragging me aloft, and only a hasty blaster-shot by Brock keeping me from being a plant's dinner.

We returned to the ship, entering the hatch a few feet from one of the vines that now encrusted it. Brock unsuited; the vine had left a red, raw line about his waist.

"The plant tried," I said.

Why?

"To kill me?"

"No. To move on. To get going. To see what was behind the next hill."

He frowned and said, "What are you talking about?"

"I'm not so sure, yet. I'm not good at seeing patterns. But it's taking shape. I'm getting it now, Brock. I'm getting it all. I'm getting your answer!"

He massaged his stomach. "Go ahead," he said. "Think it out loud."

"I'm putting it together out of my dream and out of the things you said and out of the vines down there." I walked slowly about the cabin. "Those plants—they're stuck there, aren't they? They grow in a certain place and that's where they remain. Maybe they wiggle a little, and maybe they writhe, but that's the size of it."

"They can grow long."

"Sure. But not infinitely long. They can't grow long enough to reach another planet. They're rooted, Brock. Their condition is permanently fixed. Brock, suppose those plants had brains?"

"I don't think this has anything to do with—"

"It does," I said. "Just assume those plants were intelligent. They want to *go*. They're stuck. So one of them lashes out in fury at you. *Jealous* fury."

He nodded, seeing it clearly now. "Sure. We don't have roots. We can go places. We can visit a hundred sixty-four worlds and walk all over them."

"That's your answer, Brock. There's the *why* you were looking for." I took a deep breath. "You know why we go out to explore? Not because we're running away. Not because there's some inner compulsion driving us to coast

160

from planet to planet. Uh-uh. It's because we *can* do it. That's all the why you need. We explore because it's possible for us to explore."

Some of the harshness faded from his face. "We're special," he said. "We can move. It's the privilege of humanity. The thing that makes us *us*."

I didn't need to say any more. After eleven years, we don't need to vocalize every thought. But we had it, now: the special uniqueness that those clutching vines down there envied so much. Motility.

We left Alphecca II finally, and moved on. We did the other worlds of the system and headed outward, far out this time, as much of a hop as we could make. And we moved on from there to the next sun, and from there to the next, and onward.

We took a souvenir with us from Alphecca II though. When we blasted off, the vine that had wrapped itself round the ship gripped us so tightly that it wasn't shaken loose by the impact of blastoff. It remained hugging us as we thrust into space, dangling, roots and all. We finally got tired of looking at it, and Brock went out in a spacesuit to chop it away from the ship. He gave a push, imparted velocity to it, and the vine went drifting off sunward.

It had achieved its goal: it had left its home world. But it had died in the attempt. And that was the difference, we thought, all the difference in the universe, as we headed outward and outward, across the boundless gulfs to the next world we would visit.

His Head in the Clouds

It was a quiet morning at Long Island Spaceport. The *Queen Henrietta* was due in from Mars at 1303, with three hundred eighty aboard, and that was the big job of the day. At 1406 the liner *Madagascar* would blast off for Ganymede, carrying two hundred and six.

Most of the two hundred and six had already arrived at the spaceport, and were nervously smiling at each other as they paced up and down the waiting room. There hadn't been a major spaceship disaster in the past decade, but people still regarded spaceflight as risky business.

There were a dozen private craft at the spaceport that morning, ranging in size from the heavy-duty freight boat owned and operated by Transspace Shipping to the slim two-man pleasure vessel belonging to Nicholas Rocklin, the publishing tycoon. Rocklin's ship, *Cleopatra,* was in center position on the field, its slender needle-like hull glinting bright red in the morning sun.

162

Rocklin was planning to take a brief jaunt to Callisto later in the day. *Cleopatra* was fueled and ready, and Lee Ohmer, Rocklin's private pilot, was at the spaceport, awaiting the arrival of his employer.

The ship would leave at 1352, or so said the arrival and departure blackboard. But *Cleopatra* was due for an unscheduled flight somewhat earlier than that.

The office of the spaceport's chief medic, Dr. Claude Grosvenor, was quiet that morning too.

There had been one case for him, a young fueler who had gashed his hand on the trunk of a feedline. Grosvenor had handled the job like the routine thing it was, cleaning the boy's hand with a vibrotool that cleared away the oil and grease, sterilizing the nasty wound, stitching it radionically.

"Keep that hand out of action for two days," Grosvenor said as he bound it. "Give it a chance to heal. And keep your wits about you the next time you're handling a feedline, youngster."

"Sure, Doc. Thanks a lot."

The fueler left. Methodically, mechanically, Dr. Grosvenor pulled his record card from the cabinet and inked in a brief report of the accident.

Varangi, Simon F., age 20. Fueler, third class.

Grosvenor finished his account of the accident and refiled young Varangi's card. He sighed. There had been one notation at the bottom of the card that hit Grosvenor hard.

Matric. Federal Space Academy 12 Sep 2021. Discharged 14 Jan 2023, unsatisfactory reflexes.

Grosvenor knew the pattern. A boy dreams of space

163

for years, finally wins the coveted berth at the Academy, goes through his first few months or years—

And then the tests, the tests that tell him his peripheral vision's too narrow, his finger reflexes a thousandth of a second too slow, his adrenalin injection proclivity a point off balance. That was the end. A spaceship pilot had to be something of a superman, and unfortunately not everyone fit the bill.

Oh, it was possible to pilot a spaceship *once*. The mechanics of the job were not so difficult, and anyone who had studied the manuals diligently could manage to get a ship off the ground. But maneuvering and especially landing were jobs for only a few. A spaceship out of control was the deadliest weapon known to man.

So Varangi had flunked out of the Academy after the Soph Physical, like so many others. The Long Island Spaceport, like every other spaceport in the world, was staffed with the nine-out-of-ten who couldn't get past Academy requirements but who had too much space in their veins to be able to drop back into mundane life.

They hung on, at the spaceports. They took jobs as fuelers, as hangarmen, as ticket-sellers. Anything to stay near the big ships and watch them streak upward. They took jobs as flight routers, switchboard operators, mechanics, popcorn merchants.

Even—Grosvenor thought moodily—*even as spaceport medics.*

Grosvenor, Claude L. Matric. Federal Space Academy 14 Sep 1993. Discharged 11 Jan 1995, poor physical condition. They had found a heart murmur; a spacepilot had to be a perfect physical specimen.

His Head in the Clouds

Matric. Columbia College of Physicians and Surgeons, 22 Sep 1995. Granted degree Doctor of Medicine 2 June 1999. Assigned Long Island Spaceport 11 Feb 2002.

He had been here twenty-one years, watching the big ships take off. He had never left the surface of the Earth. He had never as much as set foot inside a spaceship in his life.

Some men find second-best occupations, Grosvenor thought. He stared out the broad window at the row of hulls gleaming in the noon sunlight, and sighed. He was a pretty good doctor, he knew, but despite the Hippocratic Oath he was nothing but a fraud. Unlike his fellow doctors, Grosvenor stood in no awe of his profession. He just did his job, and that was all it was.

Just a job. Nothing more. There was only one profession that mattered, and Grosvenor had long since been cut off from that.

Grosvenor glanced up as the door to his office opened. He grinned at the tanned spaceman who stood there.

"Hello, Lee. How's the lackey of Wall Street today?"

"Can't complain. Blasting off for Callisto this afternoon," Ohmer said. "Old man Rocklin's taking a little vacation again."

"The pleasures of the idle rich," Grosvenor said. He leered evilly. "I'll bet you're mentioned in his will, Lee. All private pilots are. Why don't you give him a few extra g's on blastoff today, and finish the old buzzard off? We won't miss him—and if you'll slip me a cut I'll fake the death certificate to put you in the clear."

Ohmer shook his head. "I much appreciate the offer,

Doc. But it won't work. Rocklin's built out of beryllium steel and structural concrete. I'll bet he could take more grav than *I* could—and he's sixty-eight. Besides, I get good pay from him. Fifteen thousand's okay, considering I spend three weeks out of every month doing nothing."

"Sure it's okay—but how long can it keep up? You're twenty-six now, Lee. You've only got four more years— that's sixty grand, isn't it? And old Rocklin probably will leave you about a hundred thousand in a lump, if you knock him off now."

"No, Doc," Ohmer said, his face suddenly dark. Grosvenor reddened; he realized he had carried the joke too far, to the point of hurting the pilot. When a spaceman reached thirty, he wrote a *30* to his career too. And any spaceman past the age of twenty-five was acutely conscious of the enforced retirement that was due to be thrust on him in the next few years.

Which was worse, Grosvenor wondered: to go to space and have it all taken away from you at the age of thirty, or never to have gone at all?

Out loud he said, "I'm sorry, Lee," in a contrite voice. "I guess I'm in a screwball mood today. I didn't mean to joke about—about *that.*"

There was an awkward little silence. Then Ohmer said, "Don't worry about it, Doc. I'm not offended. I know what's griping you—and believe me, I feel for you. Hell, I've *been* up there!"

Grosvenor had his answer. Just a taste of the sky's blackness, just a few moments above the clouds—that was worth a whole lifetime of grubby doctoring on the ground.

He turned away, and stared out the window—the big

picture window they had given him, so he could watch the graceful ships as they came and went.

"You've got to hand it to that Rocklin," Grosvenor said, his eyes on the supple lines of the *Cleopatra*. "He really travels in style. That ship of his must be the loveliest private job in the world."

"You're not kidding. He poured millions into that flivver. And it's the smoothest, gentlest job to pilot you could imagine. Why—"

"Must be something wrong with my eyes," Grosvenor said irrelevantly.

"Huh?"

The doctor blinked them two or three times. "Guess I need new glasses. I'm seeing things."

He pointed to the tapering *Cleopatra* alone in the center of the blastoff field. "Seems like your jets are firing. But that's impossible, isn't it?"

Ohmer chuckled. "Must be a mirage. The heat's getting you, Doc."

But Grosvenor shook his head. "No. Come here and see for yourself!"

Still chuckling, Ohmer moved to the window. A quiet strangling sound rumbled up from his throat.

"You see what I see?" he asked.

Grosvenor nodded.

The *Cleopatra* was twenty feet off the ground, standing on a tail of fire so bright it hurt the eyes. It wobbled there hesitantly for a second or two, then began to rise.

It climbed eccentrically, but within moments it had arched through the atmosphere and was out of sight.

It couldn't have happened. But it had.

167

His Head in the Clouds

A few seconds later, the keening wail of the emergency alarm siren began to shrill through the spaceport.

For Peter Michael Willer, who was fourteen, the day had begun in an ordinary fashion. The alarm had been set for 7:45, but, as usual, Pete woke at 7, without mechanical aid. There were much more important things to do than sleeping.

He snapped off the alarm, reached under his pillow, and drew out the latest copy of *Fact Space Comics*. It showed a spaceship orbiting in on Saturn, bright ion-flares trailing from its jets, while a sister ship approached the ringed planet in a wider course.

He had read the issue twelve times—but there wouldn't be another for three weeks, and so he had no choice but to read it again.

When he was through, he glanced up at the books on his shelf—the brightly colored volumes labelled *How to Pilot Space Ships* and *Astrogation Made Easy*. He knew every word of them by heart. He took them down, fondled their tattered pages, put them back.

He dressed slowly, tiptoed through the silent house, opened the front door. It was a bright, clear morning; he squinted into the distance and saw the beacon tower of the Long Island Spaceport, and a little quiver of excitement ran through him.

The mail had arrived. Peter snatched it up anxiously and riffled through it.

Bills. Letters from his father, stationed in New Mexico working on a top-secret space project. A comic book that his silly kid sister subscribed to.

Ah! Here it is! He felt his heart start to pound as he came across the official-looking white envelope.

Mr. P. M. Willer, Jr.
43 Red Maple Drive North
Levittown, Long Island

The return address was even more exciting:

Federal Academy of Astrogation,
Admissions Office
Washington, D.C. 20006

Letting the other letters drop unheeded to the ground, he ripped it open and read it:

13 May 2023

Mr. P. M. Willer, Jr.
43 Red Maple Dr. N.
Levittown, Long Island
My dear Mr. Willer:

Thank you for your letter of 6 May. We are in receipt of your application for admission to the Academy, and have considered it most carefully.

On the basis of the information you give, I can safely say that you have the necessary enthusiasm and willingness to learn that marks a successful Academy candidate. However, you fail to toe the mark in one respect. Minimum age for admission to Academy is 18, and this cannot be waived in any case whatsoever.

Therefore, may I suggest that you contact us again in four years, when you will be eligible for admission? I'm sure there'll be room for someone of your potentiality in the Class of 2031, and I'll be looking forward to hearing from you again when you've completed your high school courses four years hence.

> With all good wishes,
> Col. Walter D. Thompson, USSC
> Director of Admissions

Peter stared at the letter bitterly after he was finished reading it. Anger and frustration nearly brought tears to his eyes, but he choked them back. He looked at the letter again.

They turned me down. He had never expected that. He had been sure that the letter he had written would be certain to get him in. Hadn't he studied spaceflight for half his life? Didn't he know the basic manuals backward and forward? They had no *right* to turn him down.

They had been very polite about it. Go away, little boy; come back in four years. *Four years!* He would be eighteen, then. Practically an old man, as spaceflight went. There would be a mere twelve years of space for him after that—and then he'd be grounded, the way his father had been, and would spend his time looking up at the stars wistfully, remembering—

Four years was too long to make a guy wait. He was fourteen, now. That ought to be old enough. He knew what he was doing. He could handle a ship!

Peter clenched and unclenched his fists. Ahead of him, the shining beacon of Long Island Spaceport seemed to beckon to him.

He turned to go back inside. It was breakfast time, and his mother would get suspicious if he didn't show up.

He handed her the mail—all but *his* letter—and ate

listlessly. You weren't supposed to eat for four hours before a spaceflight. Well, that was only until eleven or twelve o'clock.

"Have a good day at school today, Peter," his mother said as he left.

"What? Oh—yeah. Sure, Mom. See you at three o'clock."

He picked up his briefcase, making sure it was closed. His mother might wonder why he was taking *Astrogation Made Easy* and *How to Pilot Space Ships* with him to school that morning.

I'll show them, he thought determinedly. *I'm not going to wait any four years.*

He reached the corner, turned sharply, making sure he was out of his mother's line of sight in case she was watching him from the porch, and doubled back down a side street. Minutes later, he was aboard the bus heading toward the Long Island Spaceport.

Tension began to gather around him. It seemed as if the bus driver were reading his mind as he slipped the token in the slot and passed through the photofield into the bus— as if the driver were about to say, "You ought to be in school now. But I know why you're going to the spaceport. You're going to steal a ride in a spaceship!"

The others in the bus seemed to be hurling the same unspoken indictment at him as he took his seat. Peter managed to ignore them.

He heard them talking: "The *Madagascar* leaves at 1406, doesn't it?"

"That's right, honey."

"It won't be late, Joe? I'd hate to sit around there for hours."

"Don't worry. Spaceships are *never* late. Something about orbits and things; they gotta stay on schedule."

Peter grinned contemptuously. Of course a spaceship came and went on time; an orbit was a split-second affair. These people were probably leaving on the big liner, or going to see someone off.

The trip from Levittown to the spaceport was longer than he remembered it; it was nearly 0900 when he arrived. The bus let him off at the big gate.

He went through. A gray-uniformed guard stood there. "Mind if I check your briefcase over, sonny? We don't want any bombs coming in here."

Peter handed the guard the briefcase. The guard unsnapped it, peered inside, handed it back smiling broadly. "I guess that stuff is harmless enough," he said. "*Astrogation Made Easy,* huh? You got your eye on the Academy?"

Peter nodded. "I put my application in already. They said I was too young."

The guard laughed. "Just a leetle," he said. "But in a few years you'll have your chance. Good luck, too. I almost made it myself."

"You almost—" Peter stopped. "Oh, I see. Gosh, I'm sorry."

The guard's smile faded. "It doesn't bother me much. But you'd better get moving. I'm not supposed to be talking on duty."

Peter went on in. The spaceport loomed up all around him—administration buildings here and there, and the big beacon tower, and fuel hangers. And out there was the vast landing field.

He saw the towering bulk of the *Madagascar,* the giant

172

liner due to depart this afternoon. He saw the other smaller ships.

And he saw the slender *Cleopatra,* standing alone in the center of the field. His pulse-rate jumped. That was the one for him!

It took nearly two hours for him to find out what he wanted to know. Finally an obliging fueler gave him the information:

"That's the *Cleopatra,* boy. Private ship. Belongs to Mr. Nicholas Rocklin."

"And what time is it leaving here?"

"Oh, after lunch some time. 1352, I think. You playing hookey today?"

Peter grinned artfully. "I always like to watch spaceships blast off," he said in explanation. "Who's piloting the *Cleopatra?*"

"Fellow named Lee Ohmer. Mr. Rocklin's personal pilot —sort of a chauffeur. He's around here someplace, if you want to meet him." Before Peter could say anything, the fueler turned and yelled, "Hey, Ohmer! You here?"

After a moment another fueler said, "He's up in Doc Grosvenor's office, Phil!"

"I didn't really want to meet him," Peter said. "I—just wanted to see the ship. It's a standard ion-drive ship, isn't it?"

"Huh—uh, yeah. Sure."

"With conventional reaction-mass? Water-fueled?"

"That's right. Say, you're really up on your spaceships, aren't you?"

"It's a hobby of mine," Peter admitted. "I guess I'm too

late to watch the ship being fueled. It's all ready to go, isn't it?"

"Yeah. It's all fueled up. But they're still loading the *Madagascar,* over there. You can try to get a field pass and watch them doing it."

"Thanks, mister." Peter started to walk away. Suddenly he turned and said, "Thanks an awful lot."

"Don't mention it," the fueler said absently, and went back to his job. Clutching the handles of his briefcase tightly, Peter edged toward the railing that separated the observers from the landing-field itself.

The *Cleopatra* looked all alone, out there. It was fueled up and ready to go. Maybe they wouldn't notice one small boy sneaking around the back way—

They didn't. He arrived at the *Cleopatra* somewhat out of breath but totally unnoticed. The catwalk of the small vessel had been extruded, and the airlock was wide open.

Quickly Peter began to climb. He expected them to start yelling any minute, but so far he hadn't been seen. People just didn't expect small boys to steal spaceships.

He reached the open airlock and clambered in. For a moment his mind went blank—then he closed his eyes and let the words of the manuals come flooding into the front of his mind, washing away the fear.

He was inside a spaceship. He knew exactly what to do.

He grabbed the red lever inside the airlock and yanked down on it, hard. The outer door slid shut with a soft hissing noise, and sealed. Well, maybe they'd notice that from outside, but now it was too late. They wouldn't be able to get him out in time.

The inner lock opened; he stepped through hurriedly, and

it clanged shut again. He was in the lounge of the small ship.

Gaily now he made his way to the fore control cabin, edging up the narrow companionway. He entered it.

It was wonderful. There were the great plexiplast windows from which he would be able to see the sparkling brightness of the stars and the pockmarked face of the moon in a few minutes. Over the control panel was set the ship-to-Earth telescreen.

And the control panel! It was beautiful! All the complex array of dials and levers and switches, which looked so terrifying to a layman but which he knew as thoroughly as the dashboard of his father's turbojet or the knobs of the family TV. There was the pilot's seat, cushioned against the crushing impact of blastoff; there was the radar guide, there the blasting key, there the jet console. It was all there.

He swung himself into the pilot's seat. He was big for his age, but there was still plenty of room. He drew his instruction manuals out of the briefcase and spread them out within reach in case he needed them.

Then he proceeded to set the *Cleopatra* up for blastoff. He planned to circle the moon and return. *That* ought to prove to the Academy that he belonged there!

He only needed to refer to the manuals once, on a minor matter of adjusting the cabin gimbals so he would have an unobstructed fore view no matter what angle the ship took. Then he was ready.

He glanced out the viewing windows to make sure none of the field workers were within range of the jets. He saw a few fuelers in the distance, pointing at the *Cleopatra,* but they were safely out of range.

Calmly, he radioed Central Control and said, "This is

Lieutenant Peter Michael Willer, aboard the *Cleopatra.* I'm blasting off for Luna now. Time exactly 1122."

He heard astonished sputtering coming from the speaker. "Lieutenant *who?* Where's your clearance? What kind of joke is this?"

"Blasting off!" he cried jubilantly, and jammed his forefinger down on the blasting key. He felt the jets throb beneath him—and a moment later the *Cleopatra* sprang away from the Earth's surface.

From the window of Claude Grosvenor's office, Lee Ohmer watched his ship taking off. His face was pale, incredulous.

"What the hell—how—"

"Piracy," Grosvenor said. "They've hijacked your ship right out from under your nose."

"It's crazy. You can't just steal a ship. Rocklin will kill me!"

Over the siren's wail came the boom of the public address system: *"Lieutenant Lee Ohmer, please report to Central Control at once. Lieutenant Lee Ohmer, please report to Central Control at once."*

"You heard them," Grosvenor said. "You better go find out what happened to your ship. Come on. I'll go with you."

They arrived at Central Control on a dead run. Major General Mahoney, the Spaceport Commander, was pacing up and down the office, his pudgy face creased in a bewildered frown.

"Ohmer? What the devil is this? Your ship just made an unauthorized—"

"I know. I saw it take off. What kind of supervision does this place have, anyway? How'd it happen?"

176

Mahoney shrugged. "We got a message just before the *Cleopatra* left. A Lieutenant Peter Michael Willer said he was blasting off, and he did."

"Peter Michael *who?*"

"Here's the announcement, right off our tapes." Mahoney handed the slip to Ohmer, who read it through.

"Never heard of him. Blasting off for Luna? What did he sound like?"

"Like a teenage boy," Mahoney said. "There's going to be hell to pay for this." He turned to an aide and said, "Have you contacted the *Cleopatra* yet?"

"Be coming in any minute, sir. It's on a Moon orbit all right, sir."

"Hurry it up. I want to find out who's aboard."

It was like floating, Peter thought. Jets cut off, the *Cleopatra* sliced like a needle through the eternal blackness. There was no sense of motion; he seemed frozen in time and space.

But there was Earth, a dwindling green sphere, the Americas visible in the classic view. And over there— that pockmarked globe growing larger was the Moon! A sprinkling of stars lay between them.

He could make out the craters clearly, the ringwalls and the rays and the vast maria. The Moon was cold and white and dead, a fishbelly color against a black velvet backdrop.

Everything was going perfectly. *Who said I can't pilot a spaceship!* he thought vehemently. *Here I am—making the Luna run solo!*

Suddenly the telescreen before him brightened. The face of a burly man in Space Corps uniform appeared. He looked angry. Peter grinned at him.

177

"Are *you* Lieutenant Willer?" the officer thundered. "Why—you're just a boy."

"I'm Pete Willer. Who are you, Major-General?"

"Mahoney. Base Commander. How did you get up there?"

"In a spaceship, Major-General Mahoney. It was easy." Peter pointed to the copy of *Fact Space Comics* spread open on the control panel. "I've studied. I know how to run a spaceship. I'm good enough to get into the Academy!"

"Why, you little delinquent! How—" The Major-General sputtered awkwardly for a moment. "Bring that ship down instantly! That's an order!"

"Sorry, sir. I'm making a Luna run. I'll bring the ship down as soon as I've circled the Moon. It won't take long."

"You little madman! What happens if the ship gets out of control?"

"But I'm on orbit, sir! Nothing can happen. I know what I'm doing." Peter smiled cheerfully. "Be seeing you soon, sir."

In Central Control, Lee Ohmer couldn't resist chuckling as he heard the conversation.

"You've got to hand it to the kid. He's got the stuff. He can't be more than fourteen or fifteen, and he got that ship up there like an expert."

Major-General Mahoney, who had broken contact with the *Cleopatra*, regarded Ohmer coldly. "This is a very serious matter, Lieutenant. We'll have to bring that boy down on automatic. We can't trust him to land a ship by himself."

"But he seems to know—"

178

"*Seems* isn't good enough. A spaceship crashing into Earth at full velocity could destroy a city. There's no question but that we'll have to immobilize his controls by remote wave and bring the ship back ourselves."

Ohmer shrugged. "If you think, so, sir. But let him get around the Moon first. As long as he got as far as he did, he deserves to see the other side."

The danger of an out-of-control spaceship was so great that ships were designed to be monitored from the ground —that is, that an Earth post could take over guidance of any ship orbiting in.

This was done with the *Cleopatra*. Lee Ohmer manned the controls at Long Island Spaceport, after Peter had completed his round-the-Moon circuit and had started the return journey. Ohmer waited until *Cleopatra* was well in on its way toward Earth, then threw the switch freezing the ship's controls and cut in himself.

There was an angry protest from Peter. Ohmer said, "It has to be this way, son. I'll bring the ship in for you. You did a grand job, but we can't trust you to land it by yourself."

"But I can handle it! I know how to handle a landing orbit! I can—"

"Sorry," Ohmer said. "Can't risk it."

He guided the ship into its asymptotic curves, shoe-horning it down toward Earth. As it swung into the final ellipse and approached ground, Ohmer said, "Better strap down hard, son. It's going to be a lousy landing."

Ohmer flicked sweat away and glanced over his shoulder at Grosvenor, who was tensely standing by. "Get the field cleared, Doc," he murmured. "And have an ambulance ready. I'm a microsecond off, and *Cleopatra*'s going to come down with a bump."

"Okay," Grosvenor said.

"Damn these remote-control landings anyway," said Ohmer. "The kid could have done this well by himself." He hunched over the control panel, face contorted as if he were up there in the ship fighting gravity himself.

Moments later the *Cleopatra* appeared. It hung over the field for an instant, then dropped. The tail assembly crumpled; Ohmer winced. It had been a lousy landing, all right.

He arrived at the scene a moment after Grosvenor. The doctor turned to the stretcher-bearers and said, "I'll yell if we need you." To Ohmer he said, "Come inside with me. I don't know my way around these damned ships."

Peter was still in the control cabin of the damaged ship, eyes closed, face very pale. A little trickle of blood dribbled down one cheek.

Grosvenor bent over him. After an anxious moment Ohmer said, "Doc, is he—"

"He's alive, if that's what you mean. Broken ribs, internal bleeding. He's in bad shape, but he ought to pull through."

"It was a lousy landing," Ohmer repeated. "A lousy landing. But the kid would have killed himself. No one can land a ship on the first try."

The boy stirred. From outside the angry voice of Major-General Mahoney bellowed, "Is that delinquent in there? I want to see him! We'll press charges! We'll—"

Ohmer walked to the lip of the ruptured ship. He looked out and said, "Shut up. The kid's hurt."

"He's waking up," Grosvenor said. The doctor shook his head sadly. "The poor kid. He'll never get into the Academy now—not the way he's banged up. He'll never pass the physical."

But he was thinking, *At least he got there once. He saw the backside of the Moon. I never even got there.*

The boy opened one eye, then another.

"Take it easy," Grosvenor said. "I'm the spaceport medic. You'll be all right. Just hold still."

The boy grinned weakly. "How'd I do, Doc? Did I do all right?"

Grosvenor nodded. "You did just fine, son. Just fine."

Point of Focus

Federation Emissary Holis Bork was a confident man—and, if he felt a twinge of curious uneasiness at his first glimpse of Mellidan VII, it was not because he doubted his own capabilities, or the value of the Federation's name as a civilizing force.

No: he told himself that it was something subtler and deeper that twinged him, as the warpship spiralled down about the unfederated planet.

Emissary Bork worried about that subliminal reaction through most of the landing period. He sat broodingly with his eyes fixed; the members of his staff gave him a wide berth. It was, he saw, the deference due to a Federation Emissary so obviously deep in creative thinking. The others were clustered at the far end of the observation deck, staring down at the fog-shrouded yellow-green ball that was soon to be the newest addition to the far-flung Federation. Bork listened to them.

182

Point of Focus

Vyn Kumagon was saying, "Look at that place! The atmosphere blankets it like so much soup."

"I wonder what it's like to breathe chlorine?" asked Hu Sdreen. "And to give off carbon tetrachloride instead of CO_2?"

"To them it's all the same," Kumagon snapped.

Emissary Bork looked away. He had the answer; he knew what was troubling him.

Mellidan VII was *different*. The peoples of the worlds of the Federation, and even the four non-Federated worlds of the Sol system, shared one seemingly universal characteristic: they breathed oxygen, gave off carbon dioxide. And the Mellidani? A chlorine-carbon tetrachloride cycle which worked well for them—but was strange, *different*. And that difference troubled Federation Emissary Bork on a deep, shadowy, half-grasped plane of thought.

He shook his mind clear and nudged the speaker panel at his wrist. "How long till landing?"

"We enter final orbit in thirty-nine minutes," Control Center told him. "Contact's been made with the Mellidani and they're guiding us in."

Bork leaned back in the comforting webfoam network and twined his twelve tapering fingers calmly together. He was not worried. Despite Mellidan VII's alienness, there would be no problems. In minutes, the landing would be effected—and past experience told him it would be but a matter of time before the Federation had annexed its four hundred eighty-sixth world.

Later, Bork stood by the rear screens, looking down at the planet as the Federation ship whistled downward through the murky green atmosphere. *To civilize is our mission,* he thought. *To offer the benefits—*

It was four years Galactic since a Federation survey ship had first touched down on Mellidan VII. It had been strictly an accidental planetfall: the prelim scouts had thoroughly established that there was little point in bothering to search a chlorine world orbiting a white dwarf sun for oxygen-type life. That was easily understood.

What was not so easily understood was the possibility of a non-oxygen metabolism. Statistics lay against it; the four hundred eighty-five worlds of the Federation all operated on an oxynitrogen atmosphere and a respiration-photosynthesis cycle that endlessly recirculated oxygen and carbon dioxide. The four inhabited worlds of the unfederated system of Sol were similarly constituted. It was a rule to which no exceptions had been found.

But then the scoutship of Dos Nollibar, cruising out of Vronik XII, came tumbling down into the chlorinated soup of Mellidan VII's atmosphere, three ultrones in its warp-drive fused beyond repair. It took six weeks for a rescue ship to locate and remove the eleven Federation scouts—and by that time, Chief Scout Dos Nollibar and his men had discovered and made contact with the Mellidani.

Standing at the screen watching his ship thunder down into the thick green shroud of the planet, Emissary Bork cast an inward eye back over Nollibar's scout report—a last-minute refresher, as it were.

"—inhabitants roughly humanoid in external structure, though probably nearly solid internally. This is subject to later verification when a specimen is available for complete examination.

"—main constituents of atmosphere: hydrogen, chlorine, nitrogen, helium. Smaller quantities of other gases. No oxygen. This mixture is, of course, unbreathable by all forms of Federation life.

"—mean temperature 260 Absolute. Animal life gives off carbon tetrachloride as respiratory waste; this is broken down by plants to chlorine and complex hydrocarbons. Inhabitants consume plants, smaller animal life, drink hydrochloric acid—

"—seat of planetary government apparently located not far from our landing-point, unless aliens have deliberately misled or we have misunderstood. Naturally most of our data is highly tentative in nature, subject to confirmation after this world is enrolled in the Federation and available for further study."

Which was Bork's job.

For four years, ever since Nollibar had filed his report, Bork had readied himself for the task of bringing Mellidan VII into the Federation. Nollibar had returned with recorded samples of the language, and a few months of phoneme analysis had been sufficient to work out a rough conversion-equation to Federation, good enough for Bork to learn and speak.

There would undoubtedly be a promotion in this for him: to Subgalactic Overchief, perhaps, or Third Warden. Of the ten emissaries whose task it was to bring newly-discovered planets into the Federation, it was he the First Warden had chosen for this job. That was significant, Bork thought: on no other world would the Emissary be forced to forego direct face-to-face contact with the leaders of the species to be absorbed. Here, on the other hand—

Point of Focus

Bork sensed a presence behind him. He turned.

It was Vyn Kumagon, Adjutant in Charge of Communications. Bork had no way of knowing how long Kumagon had been peering over his shoulder; he resented the intrusion on an Emissary's privacy.

And Kumagon's green eyes were faintly slitted—the mark of Gyralin blood somewhere in his heritage. As a pure-bred Vengol of the Federation's First Planet, Bork felt vague contempt for his assistant. "Yes?" he said, mildly but with undertones of scorn.

Kumagon's slitted eyes fixed sharply on the Emissary's. "Sir, the Mellidani have beamed us for some advice."

"Eh?"

"They'd like to know how close to the Terran dome we want to land, sir."

Bork barely repressed a gasp. "*What* Terran dome?"

"They said the Terrans established a base here several months ago. Sir? Are you well? You—"

"Tell them," Bork said heavily, "that we wish to land no closer than five miles from the Terran dome, and no farther than ten. Can you translate that into their equivalents?"

"Yes, sir."

"Then transmit it." Bork choked back a strangled cry of rage. Someone, he thought, had blundered in the home office. That Terrans should be allowed to land on a world being groomed for Federation entry—!

Why, it was unthinkable!

The planet was the most forbidding-looking Bork had ever seen, and he had seen a great many. With screens turned to maximal periphery, he could stand in the snout of the ship and look out on Mellidan VII as if he stood outside. It was hardly a pleasant sight.

The land was utterly flat. Long stretches of barren gray-brown soil extended in every direction, sweeping upward into tiny hillocks far toward the horizon. Soil implied the presence of bacteria: anerobic bacteria, of course, needing no oxygen.

There were seas, too, shimmering shallow pools of carbon tetrachloride that had precipitated out of the atmosphere. Plants grew in these ponds: ugly squishy plants that looked like hordes of gray bladders strung on thick hairy ropes. They lay flat against the bright surface of the carbon tetrachloride pond, drifting. As Bork watched, a Mellidani appeared, wading knee-deep, gathering the bladders, slinging them over his blocky round shoulders. He was a farmer, no doubt.

At this distance it was difficult to tell much about the alien, except that his body was segmented crustacean-fashion, humanoid otherwise; his skin looked thick, waxy, leathery. Chief Scout Nollibar had postulated some member of the paraffin series as the chief constituent of Mellidani protoplasm; he was probably right.

Clouds of gaseous chlorine hung thick overhead, draping the sky with a yellow-green blanket. Somewhere directly above burned the sun Mellidan: a white dwarf of ferocious intensity, its heat negated by the planet's distance from it and by the swath of chlorine that was the atmosphere's main component.

One other distinct feature made up the view as Bork saw it. Some eight miles directly westward, the violet-hued arc of a plastic-extrusion habitation dome rose from the bare plain. Bork had seen such domes before—more than forty years before, when he had served as a member of the last mission to Terra.

He had been only a Fifth Attaché then, though soon afterward he had begun the rapid climb that would bring him to the rank of Federation Emissary. On that occasion, the Emissary had been old Morvil Brek, who had added twelve worlds to the Federation during his distinguished career. Brek had been named to make the fifth attempt to enroll the Sol system.

The mission had been a failure; the Terran government had emphatically rejected any offer to federate, and Emissary Brek then declared the system nonfederated for good, in a bitter little speech which fell short of making its intended effect of altering the Terran decision. The Galactics had departed—and, on the outward trip, Bork had seen the violet domes on the snowswept plains of Sol IX, where the Terrans had established an encampment.

He scowled, now. Terrans on Mellidan VII? *Why? Why?*

"Contact has been made with the Mellidani leaders, sir," Kumagon said gently.

Bork drew his eyes from the Terran dome. It seemed to him he could almost see the Terrans moving about within it, pale-skinned, ten-fingered, almost repellingly hairy men with that damned sly expression always on their faces—

Just imagination. He sighed.

"Transfer the line up here," Bork said to his Adjutant. "I'll talk to them from my chair."

Bork sprawled in a leisure-loving way into the intricate reticulations of the webfoam chair; he nudged a stud at its base and the chair began to quiver gently, massaging him, easing the stress-and-fatigue poisons from his muscles. After a moment, the communicator screen lit up, breaking into the wide-periphery view of the landscape.

Three Mellidani faced him squarely. They were chalk-white and without hair: their eyes were set deep in their round skulls, ringed with massive orbital ridges, veiled from time to time by fast-flickering nictitating membranes, while their mouths (if mouths they were) were but thin lipless slits. Three nostrils formed a squat triangle midway between eyes and mouth, while cupped processes jutting from the sides of the head seemed to equate with ears. Bork was not surprised at this superficial resemblance to the standard humanoid type; there is a certain most efficient pattern of construction for an erect humanoid biped, and virtually all such life adheres to it.

The Emissary said, "I greet you in the name of the Federation of Worlds. My name is Holis Bork; my title, 'Emissary'."

The centermost of the aliens moved his lipless mouth; words came forth. The linguistic pattern, too, adhered to norms. "I am Leader this month. My name is unimportant. What does your Federation want with us?"

It was the expected quasi-belligerent response. Twenty years of Emissary duties had reduced the operation to a series of conditioned reflexes, so far as Bork was concerned. Stimulus A produced response B, which was dealt with by means of technique C.

He said, "The Federation is composed of four hundred eighty-five worlds scattered throughout some thirty thousand light-years. Its capital and First Planet is Vengo in the Darkir system; its member peoples live in unmatched unity.

Current Federation population is twenty-seven billion. Membership in the Federation will guarantee you free and equal rights, full representation, and the complete benefits of a Galactic civilization that has been in existence for eleven thousand years."

He paused triumphantly with soundless fanfare. The array of statistics was calculated to arouse a feeling of awe and lead naturally to the next group of response-leads. The Federation's psychometrists had perfected this technique over millennia.

But the Mellidani Leader's reaction jarred Bork. The alien said, "Why is it that the Terrans do not belong to the Federation?"

Bork had been ready with the next concept-group; he had already begun to bring forth the second phase of his argument when the impact of the Mellidani's sudden irrelevant question slammed into his nervous system and set the neat circuitry of his mind oscillating wildly.

It was a dizzy moment. But Bork had his nerves under control almost instantly, and a moment later had formulated a new pat reply he hoped would cover the new situation.

"The Terrans," he said, "did not choose to enter the Federation—thereby demonstrating that they lack the wisdom and maturity of a truly Galactic-minded race."

It was impossible to tell what emotions were in play behind the alien's almost inflexible features. Bork found himself trembling; he docketed a mental note to have a neural overhaul when he returned to Vengo.

The alien said, "You imply by this that the Federation worlds are superior to the Terran worlds. In what way?"

Again Bork's nerves were jolted. The interview was

taking a very unpredictable pattern indeed. *Damn* those Terrans, he thought. And double-damn Security for allowing them to get a foothold here with an Emissary on his way!

Sweat dribbled down the Emissary's olive-green skin. His military collar was probably drooping by now. He rooted in his mind for some sequence of arguments that would answer the stubborn alien's question, and at length came up with:

"The Federation worlds are superior in that they have complete homogeneity of thought, feeling, and purpose. We have a common ground for intellectual endeavor and for commercial traffic. We share laws, works of art, ways of thinking. The Earthmen have deliberately placed themselves beyond the pale of this communion—cut themselves off from every other civilized world of the galaxy."

"They have not cut themselves off from us. They came here quite willingly and have lived here during three Leaderships."

Damn the Terrans! Damn damn damn—

"They mean to corrupt you," Bork said desperately. "To lead you away from the right path. They are malicious: unable to enter Galactic society themselves through their own antisocial tendencies, they try now to drag an innocent world into the same quagmire, the same—"

Bork stopped suddenly. His hands were shaking; his body was bathed in perspiration. He realized gloomily that for the first time in his career he had no notion whatever of the next line of thought to pursue.

Promotion, glory, past achievements—all down the sink because of failure now, here? He swallowed hard.

"We'll continue our discussions tomorrow," he said hoarsely. "I would not keep you from your daily work."

"Very well. Tomorrow the man at my left will be Leader. Address your words then to him."

In the state he was in, Bork had little further interest in protocol. He broke the contact hastily and sank back in the cradle of webfoam, tense, sweat-drenched.

The pouch of his tunic yielded three green-gold pellets: metabolic compensators. Bork gobbled them hurriedly, and, as his body returned to normal equilibrium, sank back to brood over the ignominious course of the interview.

Naturally, Bork thought, the conversation had been monitored and recorded. That meant that Vyn Kumagon and six or seven technicians had been eye-witness to the Emissary's fumbling handling of the first interview—and, with the interview already permanently locked into a cellular recorder, there would be many more eavesdroppers, a long chain of them between here and Vengo and the First Warden.

Bork knew he had to redeem himself.

High faith had been placed in him—but who could have anticipated a Terran counter-propaganda force on Mellidan VII? It had shattered his calm.

He would have to rethink his approach.

Undeniably, the Terrans were here. And undeniably they had made overtures of some sort toward the aliens. Of what sort? That was the missing datum. The keystone of all possible speculations was missing: the purpose of the Terrans.

Did they have some strategic use in mind for Mellidan VII? That seemed improbable, in view of the world's forbidding nature. No Terran colony could survive here without the protection of a dome. Unless, he thought coldly, they meant to take over the planet and convert it into a new Earth, as they had done with Sol II, Sol IV, and one of the moons of Sol VI. That would mean the death or deportation of the Mellidani, but would the Terrans worry long over that?

But—why would they pick an inhabited world for such a project, when there yet remained a dead planet in their own system? Bork forced himself to reject the colonization plan as implausible under any circumstances.

Perhaps Terra had some yet unknown economic need that Mellidan VII met. Perhaps—

Bork's head ached. Speculation was not easy for him. After a while he rose and went below to seek sleep.

There was a fixed routine for the assimilation of worlds into the Federation. It was a routine developed over thousands of years—ever since Vengo spread out to absorb its three sister worlds, eleven thousand years Galactic before, and the Federation was born. The routine customarily was successful.

Growth had been slow, at first. Two solar systems the first millennium, yielding five inhabited worlds. Then three systems the second millennium, with four worlds. Eleven worlds the next, seventeen the next—

Until four hundred eighty-five worlds had been folded into the protective warmth of the Federation, nineteen during Bork's own lifetime. Only four worlds had ever refused to come in: the four Terran worlds, approached five times without success over the preceding two centuries. And now, Mellidan VII showed signs of recalcitrance. Bork

resolved to use the age-old phrases and persuasion techniques until the Mellidani were unable to resist.

Violence, of course was shunned; the Federation had
outgrown that millennia ago. But there were other methods.

When the Mellidani trio returned on the following day
for their meeting with Bork, the Emissary was ready for
them, nerves soothed, mind primed and alert. Today, he
noticed, the order had indeed been shuffled. The monthly
changeover in planetary leadership had taken place.

Bork said, "Yesterday we were discussing the advantages
of Federation membership for your world. You suggested
that you might be more sympathetic to the Terrans than
you are to us. Would you care to tell me just what guaran-
tees the Terrans have made to you?"

"None."

"But—"

"The Terrans have warned us against entering your
Federation. They say your promises are false, that you
will deceive us and swallow us up in your hugeness."

Bork stiffened. "Did they ask you to sign any sort of
treaty with them?"

"No. None whatever."

"Then what have they been doing here since they
landed?" Bork demanded, exasperated.

"Taking measurements of our planet, making scientific
studies, exploring and learning. They have also been telling
us somewhat about your Federation and warning us against
you."

"They have no right to poison your minds against us!
We came here in good faith to demonstrate to you how it
was to your advantage to join the Federation."

"And the Terrans came in good faith to tell us the

194

opposite," returned the alien implacably. Bork had a sudden sense of the unfleshliness of the creature, of its strange hydrocarbon chemistry and its chlorine-breathing lungs. It seemed to him that the stiff white face of the Mellidani was a mask that hid only other masks within.

"Whom should we believe?" the alien asked. "You—or the Terrans?"

Bork moistened tension-parched lips. "The Earthmen clearly lie. We have brought with us films and charts of Galactic progress. The Federation is plainly preferable to the rootless, companionless life the Terrans have chosen. Be reasonable, friends. Should you cut yourself off from the main current of Galactic life by refusing to join the Federation? You're intelligent; I can see that immediately. Why withdraw? If you decline to Federate, it will become impossible for you to have cultural or commercial interchange with any of the Federated worlds. You—"

"Answer this question, please," said the Mellidani abruptly. "Why is this Federation of yours necessary?"

"What?"

"Why can't we have these contacts *without* joining?"

"Why—because—"

Bork gasped like a creature jerked suddenly from its natural element. This sudden nerve-shattering question had thrust itself between his ribs like a keen blade.

He realized he had no answer to the alien's question. No glib catchphrases rose to his lips. He sputtered inanely, reddened, and finally took recourse in the same tactic of retreat he had employed the day before.

"This is a question that requires further study. I'll take it up with you tomorrow at this time."

The Mellidani faded from the glowing screen. Emissary

Bork made contact with Adjutant Kumagon and said, "Get in touch with the Terrans. There has to be an immediate conference with them."

"At once," Kumagon said.

Bork scowled. The Adjutant seemed almost pleased. Was that the shadow of a smile flickering on the man's lips?

Later that day a hatch near the firing tubes of the Federation ship pivoted open and the shining beetle-like shape of a landcar dropped through, its treads striking the barren Mellidani soil and carrying it swiftly away. Aboard were Emissary Holis Bork and two aides: Fifth Attaché Hu Sdreen and Third Attaché Brul Dirrib.

The landcar sped across the ground, through the shallow pools of precipitated carbon tetrachloride, through the low-hanging thick murk of the sky, and minutes later arrived at the violet-hued Terran habitation dome.

There, a hatch swung open, admitting the car to an air lock. The hatch sealed hissingly; a second lock irised open, and air—oxynitrogen air—coursed in. Several Terrans were waiting as Bork and his aides stepped from the landcar.

Bork felt uneasy in their presence. They were trim, lean, efficient-looking men, all clad more or less alike. One, older than the rest, came forward and lifted his hand in a formal Federation salute, which Bork automatically returned.

"I'm Major-General Gambrell," the Terran said, speaking fluent Federation. The second mission to Terra had educated the natives in the Galactic tongue, and they had never forgotten it. "I'm in charge here for the time being," Gambrell said. "Suppose you come on up to my office and we can talk this thing over."

Gambrell led the way up a neat row of low metal houses and entered one several stories high; Bork followed him, signalling the aides to remain outside. When they were within, Gambrell seated himself behind a battered wooden desk, fished in his pocket, and produced a cigarette pack. He offered it to Bork.

"Care to have a smoke?"

"Sorry," the Emissary said, repressing his disgust. "We don't indulge."

"Of course. I forgot." Gambrell smiled apologetically. "You don't mind if I smoke, do you?"

Bork shrugged. "Not at all."

Gambrell flicked the igniting capsule at the cigarette's tip, waited a moment, then puffed at the other end. He looked utterly relaxed. Bork was sharply tuned for this meeting; every nerve was tight-strung.

The Earthman said, "All right. Just why have you requested this meeting, Emissary Bork?"

"You know our purpose here on Mellidan VII?" Bork asked.

"Certainly. You're here to enroll the Mellidani in your Federation."

Bork nodded. "Our aim is clear to you, then. But why are *you* here, Major-General Gambrell? Why has Earth established this outpost?"

The Earthman ran one hand lightly through the close-cropped thatch of graying hair that covered most of his scalp. Bork thought of the vestigial topknot that was *his* only heritage from the past, and smiled smugly. After a moment Gambrell said, "We're here to keep Mellidan VII from joining the Federation. Is that clear enough?"

"It is," Bork said tightly. "May I ask what you hope to

197

gain by this deliberate interference? I suppose you plan to use Mellidan VII as some sort of military base, no doubt."

"No."

Bork had gained flexibility during the past few days. He shot an instant rejoinder at the Earthman: "In that case you must have some commercial purpose in mind. What?"

The Earthman shook his head. "Let me be perfectly honest with you, Emissary Bork. *We don't have any actual use for Mellidan VII.* It's just too damn alien a world for oxygen-breathers to use without conversion."

Bork frowned. "You have *no use* for Mellidan VII? But —then—that means you came here solely for the purpose of—of—"

"Right. Of keeping it out of the Federation's hands."

The man's arrogance stunned Bork. That Earth should wantonly block a Federation mission for no reason at all—

"This is a very serious matter," Bork said.

"I know. More serious than you yourself think, Emissary Bork. Look here: suppose you tell me why the Federation wants Mellidan VII, now?"

Bork glared at the infuriatingly calm Earthman. "We want it because—because—"

He stopped. The question paralleled the ones the Mellidani Leader had asked. It produced the same visceral reaction. These basic questions hit deep, he thought. And there were no ready answers for them.

Gambrell said smoothly, "I see you're in difficulties. Here's an answer for you: *you want it simply because it's there.* Because for eleven thousand years you've Federated every planet you could, swallowed it up in your benevolent

198

arms, thoroughly homogenized its culture into yours and blotted out any minor differences that might have existed. You don't see any reason to stop now. But you don't have any possible use for this world, do you? You can't trade with it, you can't colonize here, you can't turn it into a vacation resort. For the first time in your considerable history you've run up against an inhabited world that's *utterly useless* as Federation stock. But you're trying to Federate it anyway."

"We—"

"Keep quiet," said the Earthman sharply. "Don't try to argue, because you don't know how to argue. Or to think. Vengo's ruled the roost so long you've reduced every cerebral process to a set of conditioned reflexes. And when you strike an exception to a pattern, you just steamroll right on ahead. You find a planet, so you offer it a place in the Federation and proceed to digest it alive. What function does this Federation of yours serve, anyway?"

Bork was on solid ground here. "It serves as a unifying force that holds together the disparate worlds of the galaxy, bringing order out of confusion."

"Okay. I'll buy that statement. even if it does come rolling out of you automatically." The Earthman hunched forward and his eyes fixed coldly on Bork's. "The Federation's so big and complex that it hasn't yet learned that it died three thousand years ago. Its function atrophied, dried up, vanished. *Foosh!* The galaxy is orderly; trade routes are established, patterns of cultural contact built, war forgotten. There's no longer any need for a benevolent tyranny operating out of Vengo that makes sure the whole thing doesn't come apart. But still you go on, bringing the joys of

199

Federation from planet to planet, as if the same chaotic situation prevails now that prevailed in those barbaric days when your warlord ancestors first came down out of Vengo to conquer the universe."

Bork sat very quietly. He was thinking: *the Terran is insane. The things he says have no meaning. The Federation dead? Nonsense!*

"I knew the Earthmen were fools, but I didn't think they were morons as well," the Emissary said out loud, lightly. "Anyone can see that the Federation is alive and healthy, and will be for eternity to come."

"Federations don't last that long. They don't even last *half* an eternity. And yours died millennia ago. It's like some great beast whose nervous system is so slow to react it takes hours to realize that it's dead. Well, the Federation will last a couple of thousand years more, on its accumulated momentum. But it's dead now."

Bork rose. "I can't spend any further time on this kind of foolish talking," he said wearily. "I'll have to get back to my base." He fingered the glittering platinum ornaments on his stiff green jacket. "And I don't intend to give up trying to Federate the Mellidani, despite your obstructions."

Gambrell chuckled in an oddly offensive manner. "Keep at it, then. Keep on mouthing clichés and giving them hollow arguments that fall to flinders when you poke at the roots. We've warned the Mellidani. Besides, they can think for themselves, and aren't impressed easily by big words and gilded phrases. They won't be suckers for your routine."

Bork was very quiet for a long moment, staring stonily at the Earthman, trying to see behind those ice-cool gray eyes. At length he said, "Is this all just petty spite on your part? Why are you doing this, Gambrell? If you Terrans don't want to enter the Federation, why don't you keep off by yourselves and stop meddling with our activities?"

"Because the Mellidani represent something unique in the galaxy," Gambrell said. "And because *we* see their value, even if you don't. Do you know what would happen if you Federated the Mellidani? Within a century you'd have to exterminate them or expel them from the Federation. They're *alien,* Bork. Totally and absolutely and unchangeably alien. They don't breathe the same kind of atmosphere you do. They don't digest the same foods. Their lungs don't work on the principles yours do. Neither do their brains."

"What does this—"

Gambrell cut him off and continued unstoppably. "They're a cosmic fluke, Bork. They don't conform to the oxygen-carbon pattern of life, and they might very well be the only race in the universe that doesn't. We can't afford to let the Federation come in here and destroy them. And you *will* destroy them, because they're different and the Federation can't abide differences that can't be smoothed out by a little deportation and ideological manipulation and genetic monkeying."

"I wish I could follow this ridiculous line of chatter," Bork snapped savagely. "But I'm afraid I'm wasting your time and mine. Please excuse me."

Sighing, Gambrell said, "You just don't listen to me, do you?"

"I've been listening. What's so important about this *uniqueness* of these people, that must be preserved at all costs?"

Instead of asking, Gambrell crisply said, "Close your

right eye, Bork. You're right-handed, aren't you?"

"Yes, but—"

"Close your right eye. There. Suddenly you lose depth perception, notice? Your eyes function stereoscopically; knock out one point of focus and you see things two-dimensionally. Well, *we* see things two-dimensionally, Bork, all of us. The whole galaxy does. We see things through the eyes of oxygen-breathing carbon entities, and we distort everything to fit that orientation.

"The Mellidani could be our second eye. If we leave them alone, free to look at events and phenomena in their own special alien unique way—they can provide that other point of focus for us. We have to preserve this thing they have: if we let the Federation destroy it by lumping them into the vast all-devouring amoeba of confederate existence, we may never find another race quite so alien, just as we can never regenerate a blinded eye. *That's* why we poisoned their minds against you. That's why we got here first and made sure they would never join the Federation. And they won't."

Angrily, Bork said, "They will! This is ridiculous!"

Gambrell shrugged. "Go ahead, then. Speak ye to the Mellidani, and see how far you get. This isn't an ordinary race you're dealing with. Incidentally, the Mellidani Leader has been listening to this whole conversation over a private circuit."

That was the final gesture of contempt. Bork surged to the door, rage clotting his throat, and stalked out of Gambrell's office wordlessly. Federation dead, indeed! Point of focus! The Federation would absorb the Mellidani, no doubt of it. They *would!*

He reached ground level and found his aides. "Let's get back to the ship," Bork ordered brusquely. "I want to speak to the Mellidani again. The Earthmen haven't beaten us yet."

They drove through the clinging yellow-green fog to the slim needle that was the Federation ship. As they drove, Bork cast frantically about in his mind for some argument that was new, that was not cliché-riddled and timeworn. And no answers presented themselves.

He felt panic throbbing in his chest. The first dark cracks were starting to appear on the gleaming shield of his self-confidence—and, perhaps, on the greater shield of the Federation's vaunted prestige. The Earthman's words echoed harshly in his mind. *You'll never get Mellidan VII. The Federation is dead. Point of focus. Alien viewpoint. Necessary. Perspective.*

Then eleven thousand years of galactic domination reasserted their hold. Bork grew calm; the Earthman's words were air-filled nonsense, without meaning. Mellidan VII was not yet lost. *Not yet.*

We'll show them, he thought fiercely. *We'll show them.* But the old Emissary's heart suddenly was not quite sure they would.

Delivery Guaranteed

There aren't many free-lance space-ferry operators who can claim that they carried a log cabin half way from Mars to Ganymede, and then had the log cabin carry *them* the rest of the way. I can, though you can bet your last tarnished megabuck that I didn't do it willingly. It was quite a trip. I left Mars not only with a log cabin on board, but a genuine muzzle-loading antique cannon, a goodly supply of cannonballs therefrom, and various other miscellaneous antiques—as well as the Curator of Historical Collections from the Ganymede Museum. There was also a stowaway on board, much to his surprise and mine—he wasn't listed in the cargo vouchers.

Let me make one thing clear: I wasn't keen on carrying any such cargo. But my free-lance ferry operator's charter is quite explicit that way, unfortunately. A ferry operator is required to hire his ship to any person of law-abiding character who will meet the (government-fixed) rates, and whose cargo to be transported neither exceeds the ship's weight allowance nor is considered contraband by any System law.

In short, I'm available to just about all comers. By the terms of my charter I've been compelled to ferry five hundred marmosets to Pluto, forced to haul ten tons of Venusian guano to Callisto, constrained to deliver fifty crates of fertilized frogs' eggs from Earth to a research station orbiting Neptune. In the latter case I made the trip twice for the same fee, thanks to the delivery guaranteed clause in the contract; the first time out my radiation shields slipped up for a few seconds, not causing me any particular genetic hardships but playing merry hell with those frog's eggs. When a bunch of four-headed tadpoles began to hatch, they served notice on me that they were not accepting delivery and would pay no fee—and, what's more, would sue if I didn't bring another load of potential frogs up from Earth, and be damned well careful about the shielding this time.

So I hauled another fifty crates of frogs' eggs, this time without mishap, and collected my fee. But I've never been happy about carrying livestock again.

This new offer wasn't livestock. I got the call while I was laying over on Mars after a trip up from Luna with a few colonists and their gear. I had submitted my name to the Transport Registry, informing them that I was on call and waiting for employment—but I was in no hurry. I still had a couple of hundred megabucks left from the last job, and I didn't mind a vacation.

The call came on the third day of my Martian layover. "Collect call for Mr. Sam Diamond, from the Transport Registry. Do you accept?"

"Yes," I muttered, and $30,000 more was chalked to my

phone bill. A dollar doesn't last hardly any time at all in these days of system-wide hyperinflation.

"Sam?" a deep voice said. It was Mike Cooper of the Transport people.

"Who else would it be at this end of your collect call?" I growled. "And why can't you people pay for a phone call once in a while?"

"You know the law, Sam," Cooper said cheerfully. "I've got a job for you."

"That's nice. Another load of marmosets?"

"Nothing live this time, Sam, except your passenger. She's Miss Vanderweghe of the Ganymede Museum. Curator of Historical Collections. She wants someone to ferry her back to Ganymede with some historical relics she's picked up along the way."

"The Washington Monument?" I asked. "The Great Pyramid of Khufu? We could tow it alongside the ship, lashed down with twine—"

"Knock it off," Cooper said, unamused. "What she's got are souvenirs of the Venusian Insurrection. The log cabin that served as Macintyre's headquarters, the cannon used to drive back the Bluecoats, and a few smaller knicknacks along those lines."

"Hold it," I said. "You can't fit a log cabin into my ship. And if it's going to be a tow job, I want the Delivery Guaranteed clause stricken out of the contract. And how much does the damn cannon weigh? I've got a weight ceiling, you know."

"I know. Her entire cargo is less than eight tons, cannon and all. It's well within your tonnage restrictions. And as for the log cabin, it doesn't need to be towed. She's agreed to take it apart for shipping, and reassemble it when it gets to Ganymede."

The layover had been nice while it lasted. I said, "I was looking for some rest, Mike. Isn't there some angle I can use to wiggle out of this cargo?"

"None."

"But—"

"There isn't another free ferry in town tonight. She wants to leave tonight. So you're the boy, Sam. The job is yours."

I opened my mouth. I closed it again. Ferries are considered public services, under the law. The only way I could get a vacation that was sure to last was to apply for one in advance, and I hadn't done that.

"Okay," I said wearily. "When do I sign the contract?"

"Miss Vanderweghe is at my office now," Cooper said. "How soon can you get here?"

I was in a surly mood as I rode downtown to Cooper's place. For the thousandth time I resented the casual way he could pluck me out of some relaxation and make me take a job. I wasn't looking forward to catering to the whims of some dried-up old museum curator all the way out to Ganymede. And I wasn't too pleased with the notion of carrying relics of the Venusian Insurrection.

The Insurrection had caused quite a fuss, a hundred years back. Bunch of Venusian colonists decided they didn't like Earth's rule—the taxation-without-representation bit, though their squawk was unjustified—and set up a wildcat independent government, improvising their equipment out of whatever they could grab. A chap name of Macintyre was in charge; the insurrectionists holed up in the jungle and held off the attacking loyalists for a couple of weeks. Then the Venusian local government appealed to Earth, a regiment of Bluecoats was shipped to Venus, and inside of a week Macintyre was a prisoner and the Insurrection ended. But some diehard Venusians still venerated the insurrectionists, and there had been a few murders and ambushes every year since the overthrow of Macintyre. I could have done without carrying Venusian cargo.

I was going to say as much to Cooper, too, in hopes that some clause of my charter would get me out of the assignment and back on vacation. But I didn't get a chance. I went storming into Cooper's office.

There was a girl sitting in the chair to the left of his desk. She was about twenty-five, well built in most every way possible, with glossy, short-cropped hair and an attractive face.

Cooper stood up and said, "Sam, I'd like you to meet Miss Erna Vanderweghe of Ganymede. Miss Vanderweghe, this is Sam Diamond, one of the best ferry men there is. He'll get you to Ganymede in style."

"I'm sure of that," she said, smiling.

"Hello," I said, gulping.

I didn't bother raising a fuss about the political implications of my cargo. I didn't grouse about weight limits, space problems aboard ship, accommodation difficulties, or anything else. I reached for the contract—it was the standard printed form, with the variables typed in by Cooper—and signed it.

"I'd like to leave tonight," she said.

"Sure. My ship's at the spaceport. Can you have your cargo delivered there by—oh, say, 1700 hours? That way we can blast off by 2100."

"I'll try. Will you be able to help me get my goods out of storage and down to the spaceport?"

I started to say that I'd be delighted to, but Cooper cut in sharply, as I knew he would. "I'm sorry, Miss Vanderweghe, but Sam's contract and charter prohibit him from any landside cargo-handling except within the actual bounds of the spaceport. You'll have to use a local carrier for getting your stuff to the ship, I'm afraid. If you want me to, I'll arrange for transportation—"

My mood was considerably different as I returned to the Deimos to check out. My tub would need five days for the journey between Mars and Ganymede. Now, conditions aboard my ship allow for a certain amount of passenger privacy, but not a devil of a lot. Log cabin or no log cabin, I was going to enjoy the proximity of Miss Erna Vanderweghe. I could think of worse troubles than having to spend five days in the same small ferry with her, and only a log cabin and a cannon for chaperones.

I was grinning as I walked over to the desk to let them know I was pulling out. Nat, the desk clerk, interpreted the grin logically enough, but wrongly.

"You talked them out of giving you the job, eh, Sam? How'd you work it?"

"Huh? Oh—no, I took the job. I'm checking out of here at 1800 hours."

"You *took* it? But you look *happy!*"

"I am," I said with a mysterious expression. I started to saunter away, but Nat called me back.

"You had a visitor a little while ago, Mr. Cooper. He wanted me to let him into your room to wait for you, but naturally I wouldn't do it."

"Visitor? Did he leave his name?"

"He's still here. Sitting right over there, next to the potted palm tree."

Frowning, I walked toward him. He was a thin, hunched-up little man with the sallow look of a Venusian colonist. He was busily reading some cheap dime-novel sort of magazine as I approached.

"Hello," I said affably. "I'm Sam Diamond. You wanted to see me?"

"You're ferrying Erna Vanderweghe to Ganymede to-night, aren't you?" His voice was thinly whining, nasty-sounding, mean.

"I make a practice of keeping my business to myself," I told him. "If you're interested in hiring a ferry, you'd better go to the Transport Registry. I'm booked."

"I know you are. And I know who you're carrying. And I know *what* you're carrying."

"Look here, friend, I—"

"You're carrying General Macintyre's cabin, and other priceless relics of the Venusian Republic—and all stolen goods!" His eyes had a fanatic gleam about them. I realized who he was as soon as he used the expression "Venusian Republic." Only an insurrectionist-sympathizer would refer to the rebel group that way.

"I'm not going to discuss business affairs with you," I said. "My cargo has been officially cleared."

"It was stolen by that woman! Purchased with filthy dollars and taken from Venus by stealth!"

I started to walk away. I hate having some loudmouthed fanatic rant at me. But he followed, clutching at my elbows, and said in his best conspiratorial tone, "I warn you, Diamond—cancel that contract or you'll suffer! Those relics must return to Venus!"

210

Whirling around, I disengaged his hands from my arm and snapped, "I couldn't cancel a contract if I wanted to—and I don't want to. Get out of here or I'll have you jugged, whoever you are."

"Remember the warning—"

"Go on! Shoo! Scat!"

He slinked out of the lobby. Shaking my head, I went upstairs to pack. Damned idiotic cloak-and-dagger morons, I thought. Creeping around hissing warnings and leaving threatening notes, and in general trying to keep alive an underground movement that never had any real reason for existing from the start. It wasn't as if Earth had oppressed the Venusian colonists. The benefits flowed all in one direction, from Earth to Venus, and everyone on Venus knew it except for Macintyre's little bunch of ultranationalistic glory-hounds. Nobody on Venus wanted independence less than the colonists themselves, who had dandy tax exemptions and benefits from the mother world.

I forgot all about the threats by the time I was through packing my meager belongings and had grabbed a meal at the hotel restaurant. Around 1800 hours I went down to the spaceport to see what was happening there. The mechanics had already wheeled my ferry out of the storage hangars; she was out on the field getting checked over for blastoff. Erna Vanderweghe and her cargo had arrived, too. She was standing at the edge of the field, supervising the unloading of her stuff from the van of a local carrier.

The log cabin had been taken apart. It consisted of a stack of stout logs, the longest of them some sixteen feet long and the rest tapering down.

"You think you're going to be able to put that cabin back the way it was?" I asked.

211

"Oh, certainly. I've got each log numbered to correspond with a diagram I've made. The reassembling shouldn't be any trouble at all," she said, smiling sweetly.

I eyed the other stuff—several crates, a few smaller packages, and a cannon, not very big. "Where'd you get all these things?" I asked.

She shrugged prettily. "I bought them on Venus. Most of them were the property of descendants of the insurrectionists; they were quite happy to sell. There weren't any ferries available on Venus, so I took a commercial liner on the shuttle from Venus to Mars. They said I'd be able to get a ferry here."

"And you did," I said. "In five days we'll be landing on Ganymede."

"I can't wait to get there—to set up my exhibit!"

I frowned. "Tell me something, Miss Vanderweghe. Just how did you manage to—ah—make such an early start in the museum business?"

She grinned. "My father and grandfather were museum curators. I just come by it naturally, I suppose. And I was just about the only colonist on Ganymede who was halfway interested in having the job!"

I chuckled softly and said, "When Cooper told me I was ferrying a museum curator, I pictured a dried-up old spinster who'd nag me all the way to Ganymede. I couldn't have been wronger."

"Disappointed?"

"Not very much," I said.

We had the ship loaded inside of an hour, everything stowed neatly away in the hold and Miss Vanderweghe's personal luggage strapped down in the passenger compartment. Since there wasn't any reason for hanging around longer, I recomputed my takeoff orbit and called the control center for authorization to blast off at 2000 hours, an hour ahead of schedule.

They were agreeable, and at 1955 hours the field sirens started to scream, warning people of an impending blast. Miss Vanderweghe—Erna—was aft, in her acceleration cradle, as I jabbed the keys that would activate the auto-pilot and take us up.

I started to punch the keys. The computer board started to click. There was nothing left for me to do but strap myself in and wait for brennschluss. A blastoff from Mars is no great problem in astronautics.

As the automatic took over, I flipped my seat back, converting it into an acceleration cradle, and relaxed. It seemed to me that the takeoff was a little on the bumpy side, as if I'd figured the ship's mass wrong by one or two hundred pounds. But I didn't worry about the discrepancy. I just shut my eyes and waited while the extra gees bore down on me. The sanest thing for a man to do during blastoff is to go to sleep, and that's what I did.

I woke up half an hour or so later to discover that the engines had cut out, the ship was safely in flight, and that a bloody and battered figure was bent over my controls, energetically ruining them with crowbar and shears.

I blinked. Then the fog in my head cleared and I got out of my cradle. The stowaway turned around. He was quite a mess. The capillaries of his face had popped during the brief moments of top acceleration, and fine purplish lines now wriggled over his cheeks and nose, giving him a grade-A rum blossom, and bloodshot eyes to go with it. He had some choice bruises that he must have acquired while rattling around during blastoff, and his nose had been bleeding all over his shirt. It was the little Venusian fanatic who had threatened me at the hotel.

"How the hell did you get aboard?" I demanded.

"Slipped through the security checkers . . . but the ship took off ahead of schedule. I did not expect to be on board when blastoff came."

"Sorry to have fouled up your plans," I told him.

"But I regained consciousness in time. Your ship is ruined! You refused to heed my warning, and now you will never reach Ganymede alive. So perish all enemies of the Venusian Republic! So perish those who have desecrated our noble shrines!"

He was practically foaming at the mouth. I started toward him. He swung the crowbar and might have bashed my head in if he had known how to handle himself under nograv conditions, but he didn't, and the only result of his exertion was to send himself drifting toward the roof of the cabin. I yanked on his leg as it went past me and dragged him down. The crowbar dropped from his numb hand. I caught it and poked him across the head with it.

There isn't any hesitation in a spaceman's mind when he finds a stowaway. Fuel is a precious thing, and so is air and food; stowaways simply aren't allowed to live. I didn't feel any qualms about what I did next, but all the same I was glad that Erna Vanderweghe wasn't awake and watching me while I went about it.

I slipped into my breathing-helmet and sealed off the cabin. Opening the airlock, I carried the unconscious Venusian out the hatch and gave him a good push, imparting enough momentum to send him out on an orbit of his own. The compensating reaction pushed me back into the airlock. I closed the hatch. The Venusian must have died instantly, without ever knowing what was happening to him.

Then I had a look-see to determine just how much damage the stowaway had been able to do before I woke up and caught him.

It was plenty.

All our communication equipment was gone, but permanently. The radio was a gutted ruin. The computer was smashed. Two auxiliary fuel tanks had been jettisoned. We were hopelessly off course in asteroid country, and the odds on reaching Ganymede looked mighty slim. By the time I finished making course corrections, we'd be down to our reserve fuel supply. Ganymede was about 350 million miles ahead of us. I didn't see how we were going to travel more than a tenth that distance before air, and food troubles set in, and we weren't carrying enough fuel now for a safe landing even if we lived to reach Ganymede.

It was time to wake Miss Vanderweghe and tell her the news, I figured.

She was lying curled up tight in her acceleration cradle, asleep, with a childlike, trusting expression on her face. I watched her for perhaps five minutes before I woke her. She sat up immediately.

"What—oh. Is everything all right? Did we make a good blastoff?"

"Fine blastoff," I said quietly. "But everything isn't all right." I told her about the stowaway and how thoroughly he had wrecked us.

"Oh—that horrible little man from Venus! I knew he

215

had followed me to Mars—that's why I wanted to leave for Ganymede so soon. He made all sorts of absurd threats, as if the things I had bought were holy relics—"

"They are, in a way. If you worship Macintyre and his fellow rebels, then the stuff you carried away is equivalent to the True Cross, I suppose."

"I'm so sorry I got you into this, Sam."

I shrugged. "It's my own fault all the way. Your Venusian friend approached me at the hotel this afternoon and warned me off, but I didn't listen to him. I had my chance to pull out."

"Where's the stowaway now? Unconscious?"

I shook my head, jerking my thumb toward the single port in her cabin. "He's out there. Without a suit. Stowaways aren't entitled to charity under the space laws."

"Oh," she said quietly, turning pale. "I—see. You—ejected him."

I nodded. Then, to get off what promised to be an unpleasant topic, I said, "We're in real trouble. We're off course and we don't have enough fuel for making corrections—not without jettisoning everything on board, ourselves included."

"I don't mind if the cargo goes. I mean, I'd hate to lose it, but if you have to dump it—"

"Uh-uh. The ship itself is the bulk of our mass. The problem isn't the cargo. If there were only some way of jettisoning the *ship*—"

My mouth sagged open. No, I thought. It wouldn't ever work. It's too fantastic to consider.

"I have an idea," I said. "We *will* jettison the ship. And we'll get to Ganymede."

Luckily our saboteur friend hadn't bothered to rip up my charts. I spent half an hour feverishly thumbing through the volume devoted to asteroid orbits, while Erna hovered over my shoulder, not daring to ask questions but probably wondering just what in blazes I was figuring out.

Pretty soon I had a list of a dozen likely asteroids. I narrowed it down to five, then to three, then to one. I missed the convenience of my computer, but regulations require a pilot to be able to get along without one in a pinch, and I got along.

I computed a course toward the asteroid known as (719)-Albert. Luck was riding with us. (719)-Albert was on the outward swing of his orbit. On the basis of some extremely rough computations I worked out an orbit for our crippled ship that would match Albert's in a couple of hours.

Finally, I looked up at Erna and grinned. "This is known as making a virtue out of necessity," I said. "Want to know what's going on?"

"You bet I do."

I leaned back. "We're on our way to a chunk of rock known as (719)-Albert, which is chugging along not far from here on its way through the asteroid belt. (719)-Albert is a rock about three miles in diameter. Figure that it's half the size of Deimos—and Deimos is about as small as a place can get."

"But why are we going there?" she said, puzzled.

"(719)-Albert has an exceedingly eccentric orbit—and I mean eccentric in its astronomical sense: not a peculiar orbit, just one that's very highly elongated. At perihelion (719)-Albert passes around 20 million miles from the orbit of Earth. At aphelion, which is where he's heading now, he comes within 90 million miles of the orbit of Jupiter. Unless my figures are completely cockeyed, Jupiter is going to be about 150 million miles from Albert about a week from now."

I saw I had lost her completely. She said dimly, "But you said a little while ago that we hardly had enough fuel to take us 50 million miles."

"In the ship," I said. "Yes. But I've got other ideas. We'll land on Albert and abandon the ship. Then we ride pickaback on the asteroid until its closest approach to Jupiter—and blast off without the ship."

"Blast off—*how?*"

I smiled triumphantly. "We'll make a raft out of your blessed logs," I said. "Attach one of the ship's rocket engines at the rear, and shove off. Escape velocity from Albert is so low it hardly matters. And since the mass of our raft will only be six or seven hundred pounds—Earth-side weight, of course—instead of the thirty tons or so that this ship weighs, we'll be able to coast to Ganymede with plenty of fuel left to burn."

She was looking at me as if I'd just delivered a lecture in the General Theory of Relativity. Apparently the niceties of space travel just weren't in her line at all. But she smiled and tried to look understanding. "It sounds very clever," she said with an uncertain grin.

I felt pretty clever about everything myself, three hours later, when we landed on the surface of an asteroid that could only be (719)-Albert. It had taken only one minor course correction to get us here. Which meant that my rule-of-thumb astrogation had been pretty good.

218

Delivery Guaranteed

We donned breathing-suits and clambered out of the ship to inspect our landfall. (719)-Albert wasn't very impressive. The landscape was mostly jagged upthrusts of a dark basalt-like rock. But the view was tremendous—a great backdrop of darkness, speckled with stars, and, much closer, the orbiting fragments of other lumps of rock. Albert's horizon was on the foreshortened side, dipping away almost before it began. Gravitational attraction was so meager it hardly counted. A healthy jump was likely to continue indefinitely upward, as I made clear to Erna right at the start. I didn't want her indulging in the usual hijinks that greenhorns are fond of when on a low-gravity planetoid such as this. I could visualize only too well the scene as she vanished into the void as the result of an over-enthusiastic leap.

We surveyed our holdings and found that there was enough food for two people for sixteen days—so we would make it with some to spare. The air supply was less abundant, but there was enough so we didn't need to begin worrying just yet.

We set about building the raft.

Erna dragged the logs out of the cargo hold—their weight didn't amount to anything, here, though I had to caution her about throwing them around carelessly; mass and weight aren't synonymous, and those logs were sturdy enough to knock me for a loop regardless of how little they seemed to weigh. She fetched, and I assembled. We used the thirteen longest logs for the body of the raft, trussed a couple across the bottom, and a couple more at the top. To make blastoff a little easier, we built the raft propped up against a rock outcropping, at a 45° angle.

I unshipped the smallest rocket engine and fastened it

securely to the rear of the raft. I strapped down as many fuel tanks as the raft would hold.

Then—chuckling to myself—I asked Erna to help me haul the cannon out.

"The cannon? Whatever for?"

"To mount at the front of the raft."

"Are you figuring on meeting space pirates?"

"I'm figuring on using the cannon as a brake," I told her. We fastened it at the front of the raft, strapped down the supply of cannonballs and powder nearby it. The cannon would make an ideal brake. All we needed was something that would eject mass in a forwardly direction, pushing us back by courtesy of Newton's Third Law. Why waste fuel when cannonballs would achieve the same purpose?

It took us forty-eight standard Earthtime hours to build the raft. I don't know how many thousands of (719)-Albert days that was, but the little asteroid spun on its axis like a yo-yo, and it seemed that the sun was rising or setting every time we took a breath.

After I had bound the last thong around the rocket engine, Erna grinned and dashed into the ship. She returned, a few moments later, waving a red flag with some sort of blue-and-white design on it.

"What's that?"

"The flag that flew over Macintyre's cabin," she explained. "It's a rebel flag, and we're not strictly insurrectionists, but we ought to have some kind of flag on our ship."

I was agreeable, so she mounted the flag just fore of the rocket engine. Then we returned to the ship to wait.

We waited for three days, Earthtime—maybe several

centuries by (719)-Albert reckoning. And in case you're wondering how we passed the time on the barren asteroid for three days, just one reasonably virile ferry pilot and one nubile museum curator, the answer is no. We didn't. I have an inflexible rule about making passes at passengers, even when we're stranded on places like (719)-Albert and when the passengers are as pretty as this one is.

That isn't to say I didn't feel temptation. Erna's breathing-suit was of the plastic kind that looked as though it was force-molded to her body. I didn't have to do much imagining. But I staunchly told Satan to get behind me, and —to my own amazement—he did. I resisted temptation and resisted it manfully.

Meanwhile Jupiter swelled bigger and bigger as (719)-Albert plunged madly along its track toward its rendezvous with Jove. If luck rode with us—translated, if my math had been right—we would find Ganymede midway in her seven-plus day orbit round the big planet.

Time came when the mass detectors in my ship informed me that Jupiter had stopped getting closer and was now getting farther away. That meant that (719)-Albert had passed its point of aphelion and was heading back toward Earth. It was time to get moving.

"All aboard," I told Erna. "Make sure everything we're taking is strapped down tight—food, fuel, air tanks, cannonballs, flags."

She checked off as if we were running down meters and gauges at a spaceport. "Food. Fuel. Air tanks. Cannonballs. Flag. All set to blast, Captain."

"Okay. Get yourself flattened out and hang onto the raft while we blast."

Delivery Guaranteed

Blastoff was a joke. I had computed the escape velocity of (719)-Albert at approximately .0015 miles/sec. We could have shoved off with a good rearward kick.

But we had fuel to burn. "*Allons!*" I cried, slamming the rocket engine into action. A burst of flame hurled us upward into the night. "*À la belle étoile!*" I shouted. "To the stars!"

The raft soared off into space. Erna laughed with delight. As (719)-Albert slowly sank into the sunset, we plunged forward toward giant Jupiter. The only thing missing was soft music in the background.

We rode the raft for three days at constant acceleration. Jupiter grew, and grew, and grew, and gleaming Ganymede became visible peeking around the edge of the great planet. Erna became worried when she saw it.

"Shouldn't we head the raft over toward Ganymede?" she asked. "We're pointed much too far forward."

I sighed. "We aren't going to reach Ganymede for another couple of days," I said. "We want to head for where Ganymede's going to be *then*, not where it happens to be right now. Isn't that obvious?"

"I suppose so," she said, pouting.

We were right on course. Two days later we were heading downward toward the surface of Ganymede. It was like riding a magic carpet. I controlled our landing with the rockets, while Erna gleefully fired ball after ball to provide the needed deceleration. If Ganymede had had an atmosphere, of course, we'd have been whiffed to cinders in a moment—but there was no atmosphere to contend with. We made a perfect no-point landing, flat on the glistening blue-white ice. Lord knows what we must have looked like approaching from space.

We had landed a hundred miles or so from the nearest entrance to the Ganymede Dome. I was dourly considering the prospect of trekking on foot, but Erna was certain we had been seen, and, sure enough, a snowcrawler manned by three incredulous colonists came out to fetch us. I never saw human eyes bulge the way those six eyes bulged at the sight of our raft.

Part of the service I offer is guaranteed delivery, and so, a couple of weeks later, I rented a ship and made a return journey to (719)-Albert to pick up the remaining historical relics we had been forced to leave behind—some tattered uniforms and a few boxes of pamphlets. A week after that, a repair ship was despatched to pick up my ferry, and she was hauled to the dockyard on Ganymede and put back in operating cost at a trifling cost of a few thousand mega-bucks.

These days I run a ferry service between the colonized moons of Jupiter and Saturn, and Erna is head curator of the Ganymede Museum. But I don't take kindly toward getting employment, because it means I have to spend time away from home—and Erna. We were married a while back, you see.

It's a funny thing about General Macintyre's log cabin. Despite Erna's careful diagram, the cabin never got put back together. It seems that the people of Ganymede decided it was of no great value to display the cabin of some Venusian rebel when they could be showing an item of much more immediate associations for Ganymedeans.

So they wouldn't let Erna take the raft apart, and I had

to buy myself a new rocket engine. You can see the raft in the museum on Ganymede, any time you happen to be in the neighborhood. If the curator's around, she won't mind answering questions. But don't try to get playful with her. I'm awfully touchy about guys who make passes at my wife.